# It must have been love

# It must have been love

JIGAR PRAJAPATI

Srishti
PUBLISHERS & DISTRIBUTORS

**Srishti Publishers & Distributors**
A unit of AJR Publishing LLP
212A, Peacock Lane
Shahpur Jat, New Delhi – 110 049
editorial@srishtipublishers.com

First published by
Srishti Publishers & Distributors in 2021



10 9 8 7 6 5 4 3 2 1

This is a work of fiction. The characters, places, organisations and events described in this book are either a work of the author's imagination or have been used fictitiously. Any resemblance to people, living or dead, places, events, communities or organizations is purely coincidental.

*I would like to dedicate this book to my Dad.*
*He always thought of writing something,*
*but never could.*
*I hope I'm fulfilling his dreams.*

# Acknowledgements

My book would be incomplete if I don't thank those who supported me in writing and getting published. First of all, I would like to thank the universe that germinated the idea in me to write a book. I would like to thank all the writers who influenced me by their own works on diverse topics.

I would like to thank my wife Mona for supporting me and standing by my side at every step of the way. She believed in me for all those seven years that I wrote before finally getting published. Thank you for having so much faith in me.

My brother Sachin had the first glimpse of my unedited book and bolstered me to go for publishing. I would like to thank him for standing with me till the end. I would also like to thank my brother's wife Miral, my sister Neha, who made me believe that my book will catch everyone's eyes. That gave me a strong sense of belief in myself.

My Friends Niyati and Samarth gave me the very first review on the story and also helped me in improving the language. I'm really thankful to them for making me feel confident enough.

I'm really grateful to Srishti Publishers for accepting my manuscript for publication, even when it was very raw. Thank you to the entire team of Srishti for taking up my work and making it a wonderful book. I am blessed to have such an amazing team working with me.

I would also like to thank you all for holding my book in your hands and for believing that I will deliver something new to you. Hope I meet your expectations.

# The Beginning

"Please help me, Mona. I'm getting late for the flight," I asked my wife to help me pack. She had been a bit upset since last night. After all, I had planned a London trip, but with my friends, and not her. It wasn't a joke to convince her; I had to put in every possible effort. And she had finally relented. But still it seemed she had said a yes half-heartedly, because she had not shared a single word with me since last night.

"Do your work on your own," she told me curtly.

"Finally you spoke," I said with a smile, to ease the iffy environment.

"How can you expect me to talk and be okay? You know that I can't be alone for fifteen days. I need you."

"You are not alone, Mona. See, your mom is not well. Think about her fractured leg. You told me you need to take care of her. Plus, you wanted to spend some time with your Mom and I think that's the reason you allowed me to go with my friends."

Her jaw dropped, as if I had said something evil. "Yes, but it was supposed to be for seven days, not more than two weeks. Seriously!"

That put me on the back foot and I got confused about what to say to her. She was right, and I knew it. So I was back to the convincing stage again. Suddenly, a cheesy idea struck me.

"See jaan, you know how much I love your family. Your mom will take at least fifteen days to heal and you are shifting in with her to help her out. If I am here, you will be worried about me, my meals and will end up being torn between the two places. And I really don't want that. I think your mom needs you. You are the only one who understands all her needs without her saying."

Her eyes told me I had landed myself into trouble. Her words confirmed that. "Just shut up and don't try your tricks on me. You are going, and I will be here. So better make sure you buy something nice for me." She said this and got up to help me.

You know, this is the most beautiful thing in a marriage. Your wife knows you inside out. So no need to pretend.

"Thank you, my love," I said lovingly. She was waiting for these words, I guess, and in response, started crying. I went to her and gave her a warm hug.

"Don't cry, jaan. It is just about a few days. I will be back before you know it."

"I don't know how you will take care of yourself on your own. You will still somehow manage, but what about Rajiv?" she sobbed into my chest.

"He can take care of himself. He is grown up enough," I said.

"I know, but he is so immature."

"Don't worry, I'll manage," I said, but I was not sure how I was going to do that.

Our moment was broken by sudden sounds of honking.

"Think of the devil and the devil is here," she said.

"Come on yaar, he is not that bad," I told her.

"Okay, okay! I don't want to argue on that, but please take care."

"Thanks," I said and gathered my stuff from around the room quickly.

I also yelled at Rajiv, "Stop honking, brother! Just a few seconds and I'll be there."

He was with a driver and when he saw me walking towards him, he came out of the car and hugged me.

"You seem quite excited," I said looking at his beaming face while loading my big bag into the boot.

"Of course, and I have a reason for that. I am going on a holiday after so long, and most importantly, free from the family for fifteen days or so."

"Hello, only fifteen days. Not fifteen days or so," my wife said from behind.

"Mona, don't worry. With Jigar, I'll take fifteen days only, not more than that, I promise. I'll drop him on the fifteenth day for sure."

"And what about you?" I asked surprisingly.

"That's a secret, bhai. Just don't ask me more. And Mona," he turned to my wife and said, "if dad calls you, just tell him we have gone out for twenty days and not fifteen."

"Whatever… just don't make your brother like you," she said slightly annoyed.

"Mona, I will make him better than me, just don't worry," Rajiv poked her again.

"Oh god, Rajiv! You will never change. But just take care and make sure your brother doesn't forget me."

We both left my wife behind after saying goodbyes.

"Hey bhai, thank you for having me on your trip," Rajiv said.

"I invited you?" I raised my brows.

"No, I got myself in, but you did not say no. So, thank you."

"Obviously, you asked me in dad's presence. How could I say no?" I said with a straight face.

"So, you don't want me to be with you?"

"No!"

"Driver, please stop the car. I don't want to go with him anymore. And Jigar, please don't stop me now. I won't come with you."

"Okay driver! Just stop the car at the nearest bus stop, so that he can take his luggage and go back."

"Hey hey, don't stop the car! Bhai, I was not serious. Take it easy," he said quickly.

"Listen, don't be so dramatic. I am your brother, and I know you very well," I said.

"Why are you so serious all the time, bhai? I mean, no enjoyment, no parties, just your rules and you! You should enjoy your life."

"Look, I'm not interested in your *gyaan* right now, so please…"

He stopped talking, but not for too long.

"Bhai I want to join politics. Politicians are so rich and have such great personalities. People die to see them just once," he said dreamily.

"There is one problem. Unlike you, they also have a brain and they struggle a bit, too. And anyway, politicians should be ready to die for the people, not the other way round. "

"So, you think I don't have a brain? Bhai, you don't know, but I have contact numbers of many politicians. Even the prime minister is in my contacts," he boasted.

"So, you usually talk to him?"

"No, but who knows, one day he might call me. I should have his contact saved, so that I pick up the phone with respect, else he'll get the wrong impression."

We drove to the airport with this silly conversation. We were running short of time, so just ran to catch the flight. We had to pick our friend from the Mumbai airport, so we had a five-hour halt at Mumbai airport. I was sure I wouldn't spend those five hours with Rajiv and it would be better to sleep at a lounge or do something else.

For now, we boarded the flight and took our seats. Just a few minutes after the flight took off, he pressed the call button. "I need some water," he told me.

In a minute, the air-hostess came with a glass of water.

I was surprised as Rajiv said to her, "Thank you lady, you came with water before I could ask for it."

"Sir, we know our customers well,' she said with a polite smile. "Do you want anything else?"

"Actually, one glass of water is not sufficient for me. It'll be nice if you could arrange for another one."

She didn't reply, just flashed a small smile and went back.

"Seriously, Rajiv?" He had to be kidding.

"What? I found her hot, don't you think so!"

"You are impossible," was all I could say.

She came with another glass of water and served it to Rajiv. I could see that he was trying to flirt with her and she was not interested at all.

"Can you get one glass for my brother, please? You know, it was a long journey to the airport and we are tired," he said again.

She politely went back after uttering an okay.

"Are you mad? Why are you using my name? I'm not thirsty at all," I scolded him.

"Please Jigar, be a sport! I like her, and this is their duty."

"She is not interested in you and I can see that, so just control your feelings. If you cannot control, then the flight is facilitated with a loo. Just use it and flush out your feelings, man."

"Don't be so negative, bhai. Think good about your brother, and please have the glass of water. She is right behind you," he said hurriedly.

"Thank you," I took the glass from her and smiled. Thank god Rajiv didn't ask for anything else. But after a few minutes, he repeated the scenario and both of us ended up having plenty of water.

Thanks to all the water, I got up and went towards the loo. It was occupied, so I had to wait outside. I heard some girl whispering, who I assumed was one of the airhostesses.

"If this time he calls me for water, I am going to spit in his water and then give him. He is so annoying." I was shocked on hearing this and leaned a bit to see who it was. Surprisingly, it was the same girl who had been serving us water. I saw her spitting in a glass and then stirring it with a spoon. Suddenly, a guy came out of the loo. I went inside and made up my mind to warn Rajiv. I rushed out but saw Rajiv drinking the same glass of water.

"One glass for him too," he pointed at me.

"No thank you. I have had enough water for a lifetime."

"Bhai, you can't even see your brother's happiness," he said after the stewardess had left. I didn't reply, just kept a napkin on my face and slept. It was better to stay silent at that time. After this incident, I decided to wait for Mudit at the airport and not to spend much time with Rajiv.

In a few minutes, we reached the Mumbai airport. I headed to the lounge to take some rest.

"Bhai, Mumbai airport is one of the busiest airports. Most of the celebrities, I mean movie stars live in Mumbai and they have to travel a lot for shooting and all. So, there are chances of spotting some of them over here, I think?" Rajiv said excitedly.

"It doesn't matter to me, even if I find one."

"What kind of a person are you, bhai? Just come with me and we will walk around the whole airport. We will surely find someone."

"Okay! And what after that?"

"Nothing, we can take some selfies with them and post them on social media. We will get thousands of likes." He beamed at his plan.

"Look Rajiv, I am happy staying at the lounge. So just come back here after you finish your stupid search for celebs. And please make sure you come on time."

"Ok bhai…"

He dashed off in the other direction, while I went to the lounge. I found a comfortable seat next to a guy. He was engrossed in his phone, and was looking at some pics.

I couldn't help but notice he was looking at pictures of a really adorable little boy. "Wow man, he is so cute," I ended up saying.

"That's my son," the other guy said with a pleasant smile.

"Hi, I am Jigar," I said offering my hand, which he promptly shook. So I took my chances, "If you don't mind, can I see some more pics of him"

"Of course! By the way, I am Maan."

He showed me his phone screen and we saw the really amazing pictures, overloaded with cuteness.

"I just want to have a son like this handsome kid. Really, I mean it," I said.

"Thank you very much," Maan said politely.

"So, going back home?" I asked him.

"How do you know?"

"The way you are looking at the pictures says everything."

"Yeah, it has been almost twenty-five days that I haven't seen him in person. But, what about you? Going home too?"

"No no, going out for a holiday with my friends."

"Friends? But I can't see anyone with you."

"Oh! My cousin is around and another friend is joining us from here itself. So, we are waiting for him." After a small pause, I asked him, "I am going to go, grab some chips or something. You want some?"

"No thanks, man," he declined.

I went to the nearby store and heard a familiar voice close by. "Hey, has anyone told you how hot you are? I can't take my eyes off you. We can share our numbers. What say?"

Before I could turn around to see what Rajiv was up to now, I heard a loud slap.

When the girl walked away, I asked him, "What is this Rajiv? Behave yourself! Directly her number! Seriously?"

"Bhai, I am in love with her," he said, one hand still massaging his stinging cheek.

"If you have forgotten, she just slapped you."

"No bhai, she just found a reason to touch me."

"Stop talking like an idiot!" He did not bother about what I was saying. And without listening to me, he went behind that girl once again.

"Rajiv, listen!" I was shouting, sure that he would land up in jail at this rate. He kept moving far from me. He was really a crazy guy.

I just went back to the store rack to find my choice of chips. But before that, a loo break was a must for me. All the water I had in the flight was still disturbing me. I rushed in and opened the door, and saw a guy crying in there. He quickly started wiping his tears. I was shocked that it was Maan.

"Is there something wrong, Maan? Are you alright, brother? You can share it with me."

He didn't say anything, and went out of the restroom. I wanted to follow him, but decided to relieve myself first.

On my way to the lounge, I grabbed some chips and went back to my seat, where Maan was supposed to be. But the seat was empty. I started searching for him. I looked at almost every corner of the airport and found him in a corner, staring at the planes taking off.

"Want some?" I offered him some chips.

"No, thanks, and I'd like to spend some time alone, if you don't mind."

"Yeah sure, why not? But just wanted to say that you can share what you are going through with me. That might help you get some relief," I offered.

"See, Jigar, everyone has problems in their life, I have too."

"It's just perspective, Maan. I don't have any problems… well, you can consider my cousin as a problem."

"Hah! That sounds funny, but right now, it won't work for me. Please, if you give me some space, it would be better."

I couldn't bear to see this guy crying like this. Just a while ago he had been so happy. I was dying to know what had happened. "The thing is, we both have time to spend here and sharing your problem might reduce your pain," I said.

"There are so many people here, and I am sure you can find someone easily. And why the hell would I share anything with you?" his tone had suddenly changed.

"Right! Who the hell am I? Don't you think that's enough reason to chat with me? Whatever your secrets, they will be safe with me. I don't know you and your family or your friends, so I won't even share those with anyone."

"I don't think you'll leave me alone." Maan's expressions gave me a sign that he was getting convinced. Just a little more efforts and he started opening up.

Over chips and a long conversation, he told me what was bothering him.

I heard him patiently and said in the end, "I don't understand why you are giving such pain to yourself. I think the matter is clear. I don't think any person would like to go through such pain willingly."

"I have that pain buried in my deepest core, and see, I'm still alive." After a sudden distraction, he abruptly said, "And that's the announcement of my flight." Maan wiped off his tears and got up to leave. We shared our numbers before he went to catch his flight.

I was lost in thoughts, when someone tapped on my shoulder from behind.

"Hi Jigar!" I saw Mudit and we hugged.

"After a long time, buddy! Where's your cousin?"

"The devil is right here," Rajiv came from behind Mudit and introduced himself.

After a little chit chat, we went for boarding and took our seats in the flight. All through the journey, I kept thinking about Maan. What all he had gone through! I was more curious to know what god has planned in Maan's life now.

# 1

# Maan

"Can you help me, please?" I asked the person standing at the train carriage door, trying to get my luggage down to the platform. The train was delayed by half an hour and I had to rush. To catch up on the lost time, I ran to catch a taxi and told the driver to go as fast as he legally could.

After one whole year of depression, I was headed towards my first day of post-graduation. I had decided to be open to making some good friends. I had read and researched about many colleges, before selecting this one. I had been a good scorer, so it wasn't tough to grab a seat here.

I paid the taxi driver and entered the campus with high hopes and adrenaline. The vibes of the place were amazing, and I instantly felt comfortable. And the most important thing, it was far from my home and I was a free bird.

I was allotted a room in the hostel in the same campus. I was supposed to share my room with a guy named Mehul. I had reached Pune just that morning, and did not have too much time to spare before classes began. So I kept my luggage in the locker room for the time being, to transfer the luggage to my room after the classes.

The campus was lush green, filling me with a strange happiness. My eyes filled with peace after seeing such a wonderful bed of flowers and all those verities of trees. I wanted to spend some more time in the lawns, but I didn't want to be late on my first day.

"Hi, I am Aman, from Delhi. I'm a fresher here. Can you please tell me where the first year classroom is?" Aman dragged me out of my thoughts.

"Sorry, I won't be able to help you. I'm also a fresher. This campus is huge and I think we should ask someone else for our way to the class. I was just enjoying the view. By the way, I'm Maan."

"Good to meet you, Maan. This garden is really beautiful, but have you checked it out on that side? It's greener." He was looking over the girl's hostel and added, "I think we could spend some more time over there."

I was a little confused on how he was finding shallow grass better than the lawn in front of us. "I don't see how that is prettier. It won't be my choice, but you can take your pick. Let's just go for class right now," I said.

"You are such an ass. I always end up with friends like you, who drag me to the class before it starts," he smiled notoriously. I returned the smile, sure that this friendship would go a long way. "Let's just go," he said and both of us went ahead. Other students were watching us like we were some aliens or something. Even we were doing the same. We took the third bench, the only one unoccupied. It could seat three people at a time, but Aman and

I took all the space and started asking about each other. I think most of the students were doing that, trying to know each other. The class was full, but the seat next to mine was still empty. The professor entered the class and all of us stood up to welcome him.

"Take your seats, please. My name is Deboshis Roy. You guys can call me Professor Roy like your seniors do."

Somebody pushed open the door in a hurry and was shocked to see the professor in class already. I couldn't see her face clearly, as her hair covered most of it from where I was looking. She moved them back with a swift stroke of her fingers and the most beautiful face in the world made itself seen. I wanted to pose like Shah Rukh khan to welcome her. My heart was thumping, thinking how could somebody be so beautiful!

"Sorry sir, it is my first day… and my train was late too, sir," she started mumbling apologies.

"Please have a seat and take care in future. I won't allow you in the class the next time you're late."

She nodded quickly and started scanning the class for an empty seat. She found the one next to me. My eyes were continuously observing her. She came to me and asked for a little more space. I made some more space by moving a little towards Aman. Suddenly Aman pinched me on my leg. I hadn't expected this from him, so unknowingly, a loud "ouch" came out of my mouth. I stood up rubbing my leg, and the whole class started laughing at me.

"I didn't expect this on the very first day, honestly. But anyway, I think you have some explanation for this." The professor was about to kill me, I thought.

"Sorry sir, it must be some insect," I replied.

"Surely in your brain." Professor said and without any further arguments, sent me out of the class.

This couldn't be happening. My mind told me, 'You did a great job Maan, by being thrown out of the class on the first day and in the first lecture itself. Great work!' But there is a saying, whatever happens, happens for good. I stood outside the class and thought about the girl. My first impression on her must be of a royal moron for sure.

Soon after the lecture ended, the professor left after giving me a stern look. I could sense he had thrown me out of class to make sure nobody else repeated such a thing ever again.

And then, that girl walked up to me, and said, "I am sorry."

"Why are you saying sorry? It wasn't your fault at all."

"Your friend pinched you because of me, I think," she said politely.

"Of course I pinched him because of you! A beautiful girl like you sitting next to him, and that too on the very first day of college, pinch *to banta hai yaar,*" Aman came out of the classroom and said out loud. So, the impression was not all ruined.

"By the way, I am Naaz," she said with a smile.

"I am Aman, and this is my first-day friend Maan." Before I could say anything, Aman introduced himself, and me too.

"Look at his face, Naaz. He is dying to talk to you, but I think he is not comfortable with girls," Aman added fuel to the fire.

"Shut up, Aman! Stop teasing him, and by the way, even I can join your group as a first-day friend," she said.

"Woah, this group is going to be the hottest group of our college, man," Aman said.

"Let's begin with a small party in the canteen then. I'll be the host," Aman offered and we couldn't say no. We landed in the canteen in the next five minutes. We had just taken our seats around a table when two people came waving their hands. One was meant for Naaz and the other for Aman. Seemed like Mehul and Nayra knew these two already.

"Mehul?" I asked after hearing his name from Aman.

"Yup! Is there a problem with my name?" he asked with a smile.

"No man, but are you the same Mehul staying in hostel room 704?"

"Yes, then you must be Maan!" We were chit-chatting over some good food, when we heard a blast. All five of us got worried and wondered what the hell was that!

"Don't worry sir, this happens many times. The hostel warden does not listen to the students, and to take revenge, they plant a bomb in the hostel. In all these years, no student has ever been caught for this. That's a record. But now it is not revenge anymore, but has become more of a tradition," a floor-cleaner in the canteen told us.

"Bomb! Are you serious?" Naaz said, her eyes wide open.

"Not a bomb, really. A firecracker actually, but here, we call it a bomb."

"How do they do that without being caught?" Nayra said. We were also wondering the same thing.

"I don't know that, ma'am," the cleaner went by saying this.

A senior came up to us instead, saying secretly, "Guys, if you wanna know how we plant the bomb, just come with me tonight. I will teach you. I am your senior and as a tradition of college, we are supposed to teach you this art anyway."

All of us found it risky, but we agreed to do it. We decided to meet at the same place, just after dinner.

"Only five of you should know this and no one else!" he said it like a warning, and then asked, "Can I trust you guys?"

All of us just nodded our heads. It was like all of us were going on a secret mission.

"Ok then, Naaz and Maan, you both get some *agarbatti* (joss) sticks. Nayra and Mehul, you arrange for a matchbox, Aman and I will get a bomb from nearby."

All of us were just nodding our heads. We didn't know what was going happen, but were in a clear mood to do it at any cost. The senior asked us to meet him at 1 a.m. outside the canteen.

"Guys, should we really do this?" Naaz asked everyone after the senior had left.

"Should we? No Naaz, we must," Aman replied.

"Of course there is some risk in it, but enjoyment and adventure come with a risk," Mehul added.

"We can be thrown out of college for this and it's just our first day here buddy," Nayra made a fair point.

"Of course it's our first day! I think that's a strong point and not a weak one," I said.

"And how's that the strong point?" Naaz asked.

"Look, even if we are caught, the teachers will just warn us and we can be back to normal," I said.

"And what if all this is a part of their ragging plan?" Naaz said.

"That can be a point, but if not now, they will rag us afterwards. They have a lot of time for that," Aman said.

Finally, all of us were sort of convinced and went out to buy the things which we were supposed to get. All of us reached outside the canteen sharp at 1 a.m. The senior was already there, so the doubt of him ragging us was half omitted. Only half, because there could be something unexpected waiting for us. But all of us were there with a positive mindset.

Senior showed us the method of how to arrange the things. He was carrying a small threaded bomb and a small string. He asked for the joss sticks and tied one joss stick in such a way that the end of the stick would touch the igniting string of the bomb. And after that, he asked for the matchbox and lighted the agarbatti. All of us went close to the warden's room and planted that cracker just at his doorstep.

"He could get hurt with this," Naaz whispered.

"We've been doing this for years. We know the exact time of its blast," the senior replied.

In a minute or so, he said, "Good work, guys! Now everything is ready. This bomb is going to be your wake-up alarm, just go and have a great sleep." He ran back to his room and so did we.

My thoughts were not allowing me to sleep. Now there were the least chances of being caught. The most difficult thing was to guess the time of the blast. I didn't even realize when I went into deep sleep. A sudden sound woke me up and I saw the same shock on Mehul's face too. Both of us went out to see the damage and found Nayra, Naaz and Aman already there, along with a few other students. The door of the warden's room was cracked a little and the warden was moving around tensed. A senior was watching us from his window and congratulated us with a thumbs up sign.

All five of us were on cloud nine. It felt like we had achieved something. Things don't end here. We had taken it like a challenge and we were supposed to do something more adventurous, more challenging. But this was the time to stay in a closet for a few days at least. I still remember the hopeless face of the warden. That day, I knew, together we could achieve anything. We were the risk-takers now.

# 2

# The Five

Days passed and our friendship reached a very comfortable point. Now we were planning to do something bigger.

"Guys, is it necessary to do anything like that again? Can't we just enjoy life?" Naaz asked.

"*Aye haaye,* so cute of you Naaz. It's better you don't get involved in this now," Aman said.

"She is just discussing with you, Aman. Take it easy, buddy," I replied.

"Oh my god, somebody's hurt," Mehul said.

"Guys, let's get to the point. I have an idea. Let's plan a blast in the class room," Nayra said

"That's good, but risky too. Let's just forget about the risk, but for me, it won't be as exciting as our last plant. Nayra, please use some more brain?" Aman said

"What about the kitchen? The food sucks," Naaz said.

"Can we think out of the box?" Mehul said.

"I think we should go for multi-blasting. What say, guys?" I said. Everyone agreed, but we were just five and we wanted to make more number of blasts. For that, we needed more groups like ours. Minimum three members were required in each group to complete the plan. Then suddenly, Naaz came up with an addition to my suggestion.

"Guys, can we spread the news about bombing methods to our classmates? We can even say that we were the first bombers of this batch."

"And what after that?" Aman asked

"Duffer, we need not do anything after that. People will do things on their own. We just have to make sure that they all plan the blast at the same time or within a gap of a minute or two.

"I think that's a great idea. Naaz, you deserve a kiss for this." I flew a kiss towards Naaz. In my mind, I wanted a real kiss, but it wasn't the time yet, though I was pretty sure that even she was interested in me.

All five of us agreed on the idea. A group hug later, we started working on finding some people to achieve the target. There are always some teacher's favourites in each class. We dropped them to avoid any risk. We identified seven groups, three students per group. We had a demo outside the campus. We taught them the trick well. We had a feeling of going on some big mission and we were preparing the javans. Nayra and Naaz were training the girls, and we three were explaining things to the boys. We had decided on the places for bombing too. Each group had to plan at least two blasts at two different places. So the total was fourteen, but we wanted to make sure that no one got hurt. All of them decided the day and time for the blasts.

And the day had arrived. We had some lectures in the morning and everyone attended the classes. We finished all our boring classes. A peon came and stopped the last tutorial midway.

"Miss Naaz Azim Siddiqi and Mr Maan Sahil Kumar are supposed to stay back after the tutorial. The dean has scheduled a personal meeting with them. Cell phones are not allowed during the meeting," the peon said and went back.

I looked at Naaz. Her face was screaming that she did not have any idea what this was about. Both of us were tensed. Had the dean come to know about our plan? After the class, all five of us discussed and decided to continue the plan. If the dean knew the plan, he'd stop it. We presumed he couldn't rusticate so many students together.

It was already 5 p.m. We were waiting for the dean to call us. The approximate time of blast was around 8 p.m. when most of the students would be in the canteen. The dean entered the class at 6.30 p.m.

"Both of you are our great students. That's the reason I chose you. You guys are waiting here for me for the last hour and a half, I am sort. That's the great thing about you guys… the patience."

"Thank you very much, sir, but what are we selected for?" I asked, sceptical.

"Of course, I have to tell you that. Our institution is making marks globally now. In fact, we have marked our space as far as London now."

"That's great sir. We'd love to help you in any way, sir," Naaz said.

"Delegates from London University are coming to our college and they want to collaborate with us, so that we can send some of our brilliant students to UK," he said excited.

"That's awesome, sir. Let them visit the campus. We will make sure that the whole campus looks impressive. We will make it look really special," I said.

"Sorry, my son, but we don't have that much time. They are already in the campus and they are waiting for us, so you both are coming with me right now. We have arranged a small campus tour for them too."

Dean's words brought us both to silent mode. Suddenly, both of us took out our cell phones to text the others about the cancellation of bombing plans. The Dean came closer and snatched the phones from us.

"I already have told you, no phones."

"But sir, we wanted to share this amazing news with our friends," Naaz was trying to save us.

"Do these things later please; we really don't have all that time right now. These phones will be with me until the delegates leave this campus," he said pocketing our phones. Naaz and I got confused.

We both wanted to share this vital information with our team, but the dean was not leaving us alone even for a minute. We met the delegates and made them familiar with each and every corner of our college. We also shared with them the projects made by the students. They looked really happy with our work, but we were scared about the blasting session. We had finished our college tour with those delegates by 7.30 and we were happy that the blasts had not started yet.

"I haven't seen the canteen of the college yet," one of the delegates said.

"Of course sir, why not! We have one of the finest dining places in our college," the Dean said. So all of us went to the canteen.

"I love Indian food and I think I would try some," a delegate said. But the Dean was not ready to accept any of those words.

"Sorry, but I can't let you have food over here. I mean, I have arranged a meal of your choice at a nearby restaurant," the Dean said. We crossed our fingers hoping that they'd leave the campus now.

"See, we really want to have our food over here and nowhere else," they said lovingly.

"If that is so, then let me tell you that you'll love our food," the Dean took a U-turn and turned to me, "Just make sure they serve some special Indian food. And tell the cook that if the delegates don't like the food, he won't be paid."

Naaz and I were making faces at each other, but nothing was helping. Good food in our canteen was next to impossible. So we decided to make some Indian food on our own. I seriously didn't know much about cooking, but Naaz was an expert. With much hard work, we finally came out with a few dishes and presented them to the delegates. They had just taken the first plate in their hands when the first cracker went off.

"What was that?" one of them asked, looking clearly shaken.

"There is a construction site nearby, sir. Something must have fallen. We are used to these kind of sounds. Students do get disturbed, but we are taught to learn even in the worst of conditions." I tried to save the situation. The Dean heard it too, and he knew that it wasn't any construction site. He thanked me in sign language. But I knew there were more to come. Just after a minute or so, there was another blast. Now another excuse was hard to find.

"I thought you guys were fooling us. You know, I was waiting for another sound to come. The sound of construction does not get over so easily. Sorry guys, I doubted you," one of the delegate said.

"Even I thought this boy was fooling us," the other one said smiling. The situation had handled itself, it seemed. I literally thanked god that we had planned serial blasts.

The meeting was over, and the delegates were too happy. But now, the blast sounds were not stopping. They left the campus just before the last one went off. Now we had to face the anger of the Dean.

"I am not going to spare any of the students," he screamed.

"Sir, let it go, please. The good news is that the delegates got convinced, and they are continuing the arrangement with us," Naaz said. Naaz was an expert in helping mellow down anyone's anger.

The Dean did not reply and went back to his cabin. Once we got back to our rooms, we shared the whole incident with Nayra, Mehul and Aman. We laughed a lot that night and decided to have a party the next night.

The other great news was that Aman was getting his own car the next morning. So the party didn't stop for two continuous days.

❖

"Naaz, I really got scared when the dean told me he would rusticate all the students who were involved in this," I told her while standing in the balcony when Aman threw a party for his car. Everyone else was busy eating and dancing inside. We both had stepped out for some fresh air.

"You don't have to be worried when I'm there," she said.

"Really! Thanks to you, we all got saved. Otherwise I felt the Dean was going to kill us all," I said with a smile.

"Kill you? Nobody can even touch you when I'm there."

"Woah, woah… don't take all the credit, madam. Let me remind you that I was equally involved in the plan and even I helped in saving us. And by the way, the word 'kill' always pushes me to some strange thoughts."

"Thoughts? What kind of thoughts?"

"I always end up thinking what happens to a person after death," I said, rather philosophically.

"According to me, there could be two options – Some say we become spirits and end up in hell or heaven. Basically, we don't end up in this world. Some others say we just become a part of the environment, that's all."

"Hmm. And what do you think?" I asked her.

"I would like to know your thoughts on it first," she counter-questioned.

"I think we just become a part of our environment. I don't believe in soul or ghost or anything like that," I said.

"And what makes you believe that?"

"Can you just tell me one thing? Do you feel anything when you are sleeping? I mean, do you feel the things happening around you? You won't even be aware of your sleeping positions."

"Obviously, no one can feel those things. Nor do I," I said.

"I just believe the same things happens after death of a human. He is present over there in some other form, but just the feelings disappear. And maybe there's an existence of feelings, but you don't have the structure to express it. I mean you are not able to do anything. Like a person suffers in coma… So I think, humans stay in this world after death, as a part of the environment around us."

"Maybe… maybe not."

"Now your turn, what do you think?" I asked.

"I don't know. And actually, I like this suspense. I think it should remain a mystery. If we know the end, people would change so drastically."

"As in? I didn't get you."

"See, assume that after death, there's really something like heaven. Just a little bit of pain and you land up there, all happy. Or you may think the opposite. If people come to know that they have to be in hell, they will do anything to continue living. All the people dying in this world won't leave this beautiful world happily at all. So for me, the suspense brings you a joyful life," she said.

"I think you are right. Suspense should not be revealed. But tell me something… what did you mean when you said, when you are there, nobody won't even touch me. What was that?" I asked.

"Nothing! I just said it."

"No, I think you meant something by that sentence," I tried to coax her into talking about it.

"I think we should go back to our room now. You seem to have forgotten that the Dean has arranged a factory visit, especially for our class," Naaz tried to change the topic.

"Come on, Naaz! Tell me yaar."

Our conversation did not end over there. We continued with some more stupid conversations. These small talks always brought a smile on my face.

Next morning, we had a visit to a factory that made equipment useful for construction industry. We left early for the same. All of us were tired after last night's party. Most of us were sleepy, and none of us were interested in what was happening.

"This factory visit would be too boring. Hope the food is good," Naaz said to me. Most of the other students in the bus were sleeping.

"You know, our college makes amazing food. Even delegates were saying that. So, obviously, they would have arranged for some nice food." I threw a fake smile at her.

"I don't mind having college food. But I'm dying for non-veg."

"Let's hope the college has arranged the food keeping everyone in mind," I said.

"We never get non-veg in our college canteen too. So I don't think we will be served anything like that over here."

We were taken to a restaurant after the factory visit. From outside, the restaurant looked average. The buffet was already arranged when we reached. Naaz was very happy that she got non-veg options in the meal. She ate like she had never seen food.

"Control, Naaz!"

"This chicken is just amazing. I can't control yaar. It has been long, and sorry, but I won't be able to control," she said.

"Long? Just last Sunday you had the same food."

"Buddy, when I was at home, I used to eat non-veg mostly every day. So that way, it has been a week. Leave it, you won't understand. Just let me have my food. I'm damn hungry." She looked very happy. I was not able to take my eyes off her. We finished our food and went back to the bus.

"That chicken curry was just amazing," Mehul said.

"Chicken curry? Was there any non-veg food too?" Aman said.

"Yeah even you had some. Didn't you like it?" Mehul winked at me and said.

Aman was a brahmin and eating meat was a sin for him. Mehul had made a shot in the dark. He wasn't there when Aman was having his dinner. I knew Aman hadn't eaten that curry.

"I think I saw that curry in your plate too," I said.

Aman looked absolutely shocked. "Maan, you would have told me. I don't eat non-veg food. You know I'm a brahmin."

"The items had name cards. I thought you would have read them. You might have started having non-veg," I said.

"*Dharm bhrasht,*" Mehul said.

"Oh my god, my dad will kill me." Aman was tensed.

"You can come out of it. I have a solution, but it's bit difficult. I think you can at least try," Mehul said.

"I'll do anything. Please save me from this sin, yaar."

"There's nothing like dharm bhrasht. Just chill! You had it by mistake, so it shouldn't be an issue," Nayra said.

"Believe me, Aman, you have to do this. I know how brahmins are. They don't compromise their religion. Nayra, you stay out of this," Mehul said with a dead pan expression.

"Nayra, he is right. I have to listen to him. Please tell me how I can make up for it," Aman was literally ready to do anything.

"You have to take all that food out," Mehul said.

"What? How's that even possible," Aman said.

"Just put your finger as deep in your mouth and puke. Simple! I have done it many times. Not because of non-veg, but unhygienic food," Naaz said.

"Also take a shower in cold water and clean your whole body. After that, you have to drink a few drops of the holy water – Ganga jal. Then you will be cleared from your sin," I said.

Mehul also asked him to chant the Gayatri mantra alongside. '*Om bhurbhuvah swaha…*' He continued to mutter the same till we reached the hostel.

"Yes, come on, you can do it! Just a little more and everything will be out." Aman pushed his two fingers as dip into his throat as he could. And finally, he puked all his food out. It was winter season, but even then, to save his religious belief, he took a cold shower. He even found Ganga jal from nearby locals in half an hour.

"Seriously, he did that?" Naaz asked me. Mehul and I shared everything that happened in boy's hostel with Naaz at the canteen.

"Fuck, he would be damn hungry. You should have brought him here to have some food," Naaz said.

"Your great Maan asked him to keep a one-day fast too," Mehul said. We all started laughing. But slowly, my laughter stopped and my eyes got stuck on Naaz's face. She was so beautiful. That again brought a little smile on my face. It felt like there was no one else there, except her. I wanted to stop time. Naaz! Why the hell was she so beautiful?

Nayra, Aman, Mehul, Naaz and I were now best friends. But I guess, this friendship was taking us somewhere else.

# 3

# Something like Love

Our bond was strengthening with every day. Exams, fun, fights – everything together. Above all this, we were good rankers in college too. All five of us were spending most of our time together. We figured out the spark between Aman and Nayra. Hopefully, a love story was growing between them. May be there was a small spark between me and Naaz too, but their spark was more visible. The rest of us knew that both of them were in love with each other, but they were not accepting it.

"Naaz, I think we should help them?" I said.

"Who?"

"Duffer, help Aman and Nayra. Don't you think they are in love?"

"You guys help each other first," Mehul said in between.

"Shut up yaar, there is nothing between us, and never say that again." Naaz got annoyed.

"Calm down, Naaz! Why are you listening to him? He is just talking nonsense. Don't you know that?" I said.

"Ha ha ha ha… I'm sorry, but just look at his face, Maan. Even his mom wouldn't have been so angry on him. Mehul, I wasn't expecting such an impact of my joke," Naaz said.

"I don't want to spend even a fraction of a second with you," Mehul got up and went to his room.

"Listen Mehul yaar… You are impossible, Naaz," I said.

"Leave him Maan, he is going to be okay. Let's think what we can do for Nayra and Aman."

"I think, first we need to find out whether they are actually in love with each other or not, because I can't trust Aman," I said.

"I think you are right, but what's the way to find that out?"

"I don't have a clear idea, but I'm sure that Aman won't talk to me. So you should go to him and I would go to Nayra. Let's ask them directly what they think about each other," Naaz suggested and we went to both of them.

They were having a walk in the college campus. It was around 8 p.m. We joined them for a walk. We did some small talk and then decided to go out for some ice cream. Aman took out his car, Naaz and I both took the back seat, so that Nayra could have the front seat. I was thinking really hard to get some idea out.

"Hey Aman, I know this is your favourite place for ice cream. But I want something new from a nearby shop," I said, with a plan formulating in my head.

"Okay, then let's go there, I don't mind."

"No no! Aman, you and Naaz stay here, I will go with Nayra and bring my own ice cream. You two just wait here."

"That's a great idea, Maan," Naaz said with visible excitement.

"Okay! But why are you so excited about it, Naaz? What kind of an idea are you talking about?" Aman said surprised.

"Leave it na, Aman. She is like that, always over-enthusiastic. Let's go, Nayra, we will be right back." I just twisted the matter and took Nayra with me.

❖

"Nayra, what do you think about Aman?" We started our conversation while walking to another shop.

"Why are you asking such a weird question?"

"Nothing, just want to say that he is nice guy and lovable, right?"

"Yeah, so?"

"No, I mean, that's the reason we are good friends… we stay together, we go out together, anybody can fall in love with him."

"Stop boring me, Maan. Come to the point! Wait a minute! Let me make it clear that he is straight and not interested in guys, okay?"

"Shut up yaar! Stop thinking all this nonsense. I just directly wanted to ask you if you are interested in him or not, because we feel that both of you are in love."

"What are you saying? There's nothing like that. We are just good friends," Nayra said. I crossed her way and stood right opposite her, stopping her midway.

"Look at me Nayra!" I said, holding her shoulders.

"Maan please, I told you I don't love him," she said looking at me in the eyes.

"Your eyes don't say so, Nayra, I definitely know that you love him, you like to spend time with him. I want to know why you are hiding your feelings."

"I am not sure about him, Maan. I don't even know what he thinks about me."

"I know that he loves you equally."

"But the thing is different Maan, you won't get it."

"Why won't I? You can share anything with me. You are making me feel like an outsider."

"Maan, I am getting married to someone," she said and started walking again. I just watched her going away and took a pause for a few seconds.

"What? I mean with whom? And when?" I followed her.

"Maan, I am from a middle class family, and there is a friend of mine from school time. He always takes care of me and my family. He helped me in my further studies too, and also paid my college fees. After completing my college, I am getting married to him."

"Do you love him?"

"He proposed to me a year back, and he was a good friend, we had a good tuning, so I said yes to him."

"You haven't answered my question Nayra. Do you love him?"

"No, I don't love him, Maan. It's just that I can't say no to him," she got aggressive.

"Just calm down. I think I have a solution."

"Maan, I don't think there's any solution to it."

"You said he is a good guy and a very good friend of yours. Then he might not have a problem even if you love someone else. Have you ever talked to him about Aman? If not, then talk now," I took her phone from her purse and offered her to call the guy.

"Are you mad, Maan? It's not that easy." She snatched back the phone.

"It's easy Nayra. You just have to try." I held her from her arms and convinced her to call her fiancé. She went a few steps away from me. I couldn't hear her voice, but I could see her. My fingers were crossed, hopping for the best for my friends.

In a few minutes, she turned back. Tears were flooding her eyes. I was sure her friend would have blasted her and might have rejected her request of marrying someone else. She started running towards me and hugged me.

"Thank you, Maan. Thank you very much, He does not have any issue with me being with Aman. He said my happiness is his first priority."

"Stop Nayra! You are going to make me cry. And maybe another surprise is waiting for you," I wiped off my tears and said.

We finally took our ice creams with us and went back to Aman. I was pretty sure that Naaz might have convinced Aman to propose to Nayra by now. As soon as we reached there, Aman went down on his knees with a half-eaten chocolate ice cream cone in his hand.

"Accept my love by eating this ice cream smeared with my saliva."

What! That was the worst, and the most gross proposal ever.

And what did I see! Nayra just took that cone from his hand and threw that on the road. She pulled Aman up by his collar and kissed him hard, saying that she would like to have his saliva directly instead.

Naaz named them 'dirty guys' and turned back, keeping one hand over my eyes.

"Are you done, guys?" Naaz asked.

"Not yet, Naaz. I think we need some more alone time," Aman said in some different mood.

"Okay, both of you enjoy. We will be back," Naaz said.

"Wait Naaz, where are you going?" I unknowingly followed her.

"Just come with me. I'll take you to a beautiful place." I did not have a choice. I just blindly followed her. There was a very small hillock behind that ice cream shop. She took me behind the shop and I was kind of scared about what she wanted to do. There were some steps there, leading to a temple, according to the sign board.

"See Naaz, right now, I am not in a mood to go to any temple. You being a Muslim wouldn't want to go, especially so late in the night too, I guess? You are making me nervous," I said.

"Duffer! Why can't you be quiet for some time and just follow me?"

"Yaar, but there are so many steps," I complained. But she didn't answer anything, and without any choice I blindly followed her. When we were just a few steps away from the temple, Naaz suddenly took a right turn instead of going straight.

"Naaz, the temple is there," I shouted.

"I know! If you really want to go to the temple, you may. I will be waiting behind the temple."

"No, just wait. I can't leave you alone like this. I don't even see any lights over there."

"I'm not a small girl who you have to watch over. Just follow me!"

I didn't know where the hell this girl was getting so much of energy from. I was literally broken to bits.

"It's quite dark, Naaz. Are you sure we should be here?" She didn't say a word, and kept walking. So I followed her. She finally settled down on one big rock, and so did I. I was amazed at the great view of the city we got from that point. I didn't even know about the existence of this place.

"You know, Maan, I love this place. It's such a perfect mix of nature and modernity. See those tiny cars and lights of the huge buildings? And at the same time, the beautiful stars and moon, and those small hillocks… all this adds an extra beauty to this place."

I didn't care about the city, I was just looking at her. Some lights were giving her face a strange glow. A slow wind was ruffling her hair. Her movements, expressions, everything seemed to be happening in slow motion. This place was her favourite and it had become mine too. If I would have come alone to that place, then I might have not liked it as much. But her presence added five stars to the place.

"I feel the wind wants to say something to us, Naaz. And I'm dying to know what it is whispering. We are away from the city, yet within the city… even I love this place," I said and leaned my head on her shoulder. I didn't know why I did that. I liked her, but was not sure if I was in love with her or not.

She didn't object to my leaning on her and said, "You are right, Maan. I feel relaxed by being here. This is the third time I am coming here. And I figured out this place as the best place for me to unwind. When I'm happy or sad, I come over here and share my feelings with this beautiful moon," she said.

"Why the moon? I mean, there are many humans around. You can share your feelings with anyone." I pulled my head back up and asked her.

"Because the moon never argues with you, he always listens. And keeps your secret safe. I get a little privacy over here. So, I can share anything."

"Even Aman and Nayra need some privacy. I think I should suggest them this place."

"All men are the same." Her tone suddenly changed. "The same thoughts all the time." I was slightly taken aback. "And let me make it clear, that this is my private place, and you are not allowed to bring anyone else over here."

"Then why did you bring *me* here?"

"Because you are my best friend and I wanted to spend some time with my best friend. I couldn't figure out a better place than this. If you are getting any wrong signals, then just take a break, Maan. Nothing like that is going to happen."

I smiled and we continued chatting for close to an hour or so. Then it was time to go back. Honestly, for me, this was the beginning of the real feeling of love, but still I was not sure about it. All this was very new to me.

# 4

# The Marriage Proposal

"Please Maan, at least have a look at the photograph!" I had just got free of the lecture when my mom called.

"Not at all, Mom. Please stop sending me photographs. You have sent me around fifty photographs and now I'm tired," I yelled at her.

"My son, they were not good at all. This one is special. Just have a look, for my sake. Please."

"Mom, please disconnect the call. I'm not ready for marriage, I have told you so many times. Let me focus on my studies first."

Naaz was standing close to me and was staring at me with surprise. "Why are you being so aggressive with your mom?" she said.

"Why are you taking so much interest?" I snapped back, still haunted by the phone call.

"Fifty photographs? Really? Are you a celebrity or what? Who sends so many marriage proposals?" Her tone pinched me.

"Mind your language, Naaz. I know I'm not from an influential family, but I am a well educated person, and in my community, there are very few educated people. Maybe that's the reason behind so many proposals."

"I get it, but fifty girls! And you rejected them all?" Now her eyes were wide open.

"Yaar, my dad arranged all this for me. He knew I was going to be at home for a week last month, and he wanted me to select a few girls from those pictures. He also arranged meetings with a few. And please don't say I rejected them all. I just got confused and couldn't choose any."

"So, you rejected all of them?" Naaz asked.

"Yeah, what could I have done? Anyway, I don't want to get married so early."

"Hmm, but just because of that, you can't hurt someone's sentiments. You could at least see the picture. And if you want any help in selection, you can share those pics with me."

"Just go to hell!" I said and started walking towards my room.

Men are men! As soon as I went to my room, I took my phone out and checked mom's message. I enlarged the picture and realised the girl was just amazing. I mean, she was easily the prettiest girl I had seen so far. But no, no. I didn't want to get married so early. My mind started arguing – What if you don't get such a beautiful proposal in future? Her name was Kiara. Nice name too. Whatever! I was sure I didn't want to marry so soon.

"So, how's the girl?" Naaz called me up while I was still looking at the pic.

"Which one?"

"You have just seen the pic. That one!"

"How did you know? Anyway, I already told you that I am not getting married so soon, okay? So please stop taking interest in my life."

"OMG, anger! That means you liked the pic, otherwise you would have started denigrating her."

"Naaz, I don't want to talk to you okay." A strange shyness came over me when she asked all this. Only six months of college were left. Even though I hadn't been able to figure out if I loved Naaz or not, this marriage proposal added some more confusion to my life.

I gave another stupid logic to my mind that Naaz was a Muslim girl and my family won't accept her at all. And who knows, Naaz might not be feeling the same for me. So it was better to get at least engaged to avoid some social and mental confusion.

I agreed on my thoughts and called my mom. I told her to set up a meeting with this girl on next Sunday. I didn't share the news with anyone else around me. Just kept that secret with me. I was very much excited to meet Kiara, and at the same time, a bit nervous and tensed too.

The whole week was going to be a bit difficult. My mind was saying no to this relationship, but something was attracting me towards Kiara. I tried to stay away from Naaz the whole week. Physically, I managed it for some days somehow; but mentally, I was unable to do so. So much confusion was going on in my mind.

"Hey, Naaz! I want to meet you. Right now," I finally called her the day before I was leaving for home to avoid those nasty fights going on in my mind. Avoiding her was disturbing me a lot.

"What's so urgent, Maan?"

"Nothing! It's just that we haven't talked since long, so I just called you."

"Yeah, tell me!"

"Not over phone, silly. I want to meet."

We decided to meet at the canteen.

"Happy? Now tell me what you want to say." Her high-pitched voice was making me uncomfortable. There were too many people in the canteen and I didn't know how to start the conversation.

"Stop shouting yaar! Why are you so angry?" I asked Naaz.

"You are asking me? You have been avoiding me for the last few days. And don't you dare tell me you were not." She was really angry.

"I won't deny that, but I was honestly busy somewhere."

"Fine then! be busy for a lifetime, I'm leaving," she got up and started walking away.

"Naaz, I'm sorry." But she did not stop. "I'm going to meet that girl." I stood up and said. Listening to that, she turned back and came closer.

"Which one, that photo girl?" Her expression had changed. Now she was quite excited to know. I just nodded my head in a yes. And she added, "Duffer, I knew you'd like her. Just show me her pic." To my surprise, she looked pretty happy with this news. That made it clear that she hadn't thought anything beyond friendship with me.

I showed her Kiara's picture and even she admitted that I won't find a better option. I was happy because all my assumptions were proving to be wrong. Naaz was not at all interested in me. But why was I feeling bad about moving on with someone else?

Anyway, I decided to forget it and focus on my future. Next morning, I left early for home, thinking all the way about Naaz, who had been such a good friend all these years.

"Mom, I'm home!" I announced as I entered through the main door. Mom was busy cooking in the kitchen. She left what she was doing and ran towards me to welcome me.

"Go and get ready! I have made your favourite food." Mom knows my choice and I was beaming in happiness to see that everything was ready. I didn't listen to her and directly took a chair at the dining table. I grabbed a piece of samosa and opened my mouth to bite into its delicious crispy corner. But Mom snatched it back from me.

"I told you to get ready first. Kiara is coming with her family, and I don't want them to carry a bad image of you." She pushed me towards the washroom to get ready. Even I gave myself some more time to impress the guests, especially Kiara.

Kiara was not the first girl I was going to meet for marriage. But this time, the feeling was different. To get a positive answer from them, I had to look well and behave well. The buzzing of my phone brought me back from my thoughts.

Naaz was video-calling. "OMG! Look at you! You haven't looked so handsome in the last two years. My god, I never noticed you earlier." She was smiling ear to ear.

"What if you had noticed?" I played along.

"I would have proposed to you."

"It's not too late; you can do it now."

"Never with you." She made a face. "I know you too well, you monster." She laughed.

"Oh, now you see a monster in me? Don't forget, you spend most of your time with me in college."

"Okay, so you think like that hah? Then you are wrong! I spend maximum time with someone else."

"With whom?" That got me thinking.

"Why should I tell you that?"

"Okay, don't tell me! Why should I even bother? Mom's calling me, gotta go."

"Ooooh, so you are so dressed up to meet Kiara. Best of luck, my dear friend."

"Thank you sweetheart!"

"Yuk!! Never your sweetheart."

"Ha ha ha ha."

We both ended the call with laughter. It was a refreshing call for me. I was sure she would call me again to check how the meeting had gone. Then, I went to my mother.

"Stop shouting, Maa. I am ready. How do I look?"

"I don't want you to be late at all, that's the reason why I was shouting, and about your looks!! Let me check… kind of okay okay." She walked around me and gave her opinion.

"Is there anything missing?" I asked.

"Yes, your smile. Keep a smiling face," she said lovingly. As if on cue, the doorbell rang. My mom opened the door. I could see some people entering the house. I was standing with my mom, welcoming everyone. Kiara's mom, dad, her uncle, aunty, her cousins and who not! Wait a minute, I couldn't see Kiara.

"Kiara, get the blue parcel, please," one of the people from the group turned around and called out to her.

"We brought some gifts for your family," someone from the group told us. I could see a girl carrying some gifts in her hands. Must be Kiara! But I was unable to see her face clearly because of those gifts. She was balancing and at the same time, moving towards me. I was standing just next to the door.

"Go and help her!" Mom said.

I was walking towards her and she tripped on the small shift in floor height while entering. I ran to save her, but couldn't reach her in time. She fell flat on her face. I had missed the typical movie scene. The whole veranda was now full of gifts. Now I was able to see her face clearly too. I couldn't take my eyes off her. Such a beautiful face! She got up quickly and started dusting her clothes.

"I am Maan, hi!" I offered my hand to help her.

"Thank you Maan. I am Kiara." She smiled.

"Ya, I know, I have seen your pic. But you look quite different in the pic."

"Should I take that as a compliment or…?" We were picking up the gifts together.

"You can take it as a compliment, of course." We went inside with our hands full of gifts.

"Why so many gifts, there wasn't the need," my mom said with a smile on her face. And without their yes or no, she just took them in her hands.

"Maan, take all the gifts to that room, and take Kiara with you," she said. It was so annoying. How easily she had said that, while my face went red with shyness. I took Kiara with me anyway.

"Don't be so embarrassed. All moms are like that only," Kiara said, making me comfortable.

"Thanks for understanding Kiara, and you know what, we are going to make a good pair."

"You are too fast in judging someone. I would say you should take some time."

"You may be right, but the people who understand my parents might be few."

"I respect elders a lot," she said.

I nodded and asked her, "You are a psychologist, I read in your profile. Then why me? I mean, you could have found someone in your own profession, some doctor too maybe."

"Yeah, I would have found doctors, but I believe my dad more than anyone. He knows what is best for me. And truly speaking, I'm not interested in doctors at all," she said.

"So, basically you are your daddy's girl."

"You are really too quick to judge people. But this time, you are right. Yes, I'm my daddy's girl. We have many things in common. Our choices are similar too. And I'm proud of that."

"That sounds great! Even I would like to admit that I'm a mumma's boy." We laughed a little and continued talking.

"Thanks for taking out time to meet. Shall we go now? Everyone must be waiting for us," she said.

We went outside and spoke to others too. It was then time for an amazing dinner. I observed Kiara a lot; she helped my mom in the kitchen without being asked to. I could see that even mom was happy with her. It seemed like she was a perfect match for the family too. Both the families said goodbyes after dinner.

I was a bit amazed, honestly. Not a single call from Naaz the whole day. I remembered her sentence that she spent most of her time with someone else, and not me. So I called her up.

"Oye stupid, duffer! Where are you?"

"I told you, I have someone to spend time with."

"Tell me, who's that?"

"Leave that! Tell me about your meeting. What happened?" She sounded very excited.

"Why should I tell you anything? You stay busy with that someone else."

"Maan, now you are making me angry."

"She said yes," was all I could say.

"OMG, seriously? I want to meet her, and congratulations duffer! Don't forget to come with a full wallet, you are going to lose some money."

"Calm down, Naaz! We have just agreed on further meetings. We need to spend more time with each other," I told her.

"Shut up! Don't be so nice. I know you are going crazy right now and dying to meet her again."

"Oh really, Naaz? I think *you* are being crazy right now and we should stop our conversation here."

"I can imagine you blushing, my poor puppy." She was in a mood to pull my leg. And was succeeding in that. My face was red and a long smile was pasted on my face. I was not able to speak, so I just disconnected the call. A new person, a new life, a new environment was going to build up around me. I was excited for my future life. But you never know when life takes a turn.

# 5

# The Turning Point

The sun was disturbing my sleep. I kept a pillow on my face to get rid of that. If not the sun, then the phone was sure to disturb my sleep. And guess who it was!

"Naaz! Why are you calling so early yaar? You know I don't like anybody calling me so early."

"And I know even then you'll pick every call." She laughed.

"Is there an emergency? You know that I came back late night. "

"No emergency, just called to say good morning." I just controlled my anger and disconnected the call. I tried for some more time to go back to sleep, but could not.

Time was passing like an express train. Our group was struggling nowadays. Aman and Nayra were busy with themselves, I got busy with Kiara and her calls, Naaz managed herself by being with her special friend. After so many investigations, I came to know that the special friends were her books. Now only Mehul was left out, and he became the one who knew the most about everyone.

"Maan, don't you think we were too good last year? You know, I feel like something's missing now, especially that silent love between you and Naaz."

"Mehul, I think you don't have any work to do now, so please stop talking nonsense."

"Oh, so now I'm speaking nonsense? You are still talking to Naaz every day, so a little bit of teasing is valid."

"I talk with you every day, Mehul. Does that mean the same?"

"Well, if we just separate, and even before I reach my room, I call you and talk about some pointless thing for at least half an hour, then you can say the same about us."

"Just shut up yaar! Stop digging those same old things. Earlier, I wasn't sure about this, but now I am pretty sure that there's nothing like love between us. We are just good friends and not more than that. I am very happy with Kiara."

"Okay, I accept the bit about nothing like love. But just want you to check your call history and tell me with whom you have talked more in the last four months."

"I know it's Naaz, and that's because we live nearby and we do share our books and all. And why the hell am I giving you any explanations?"

"Okay, just leave it! You are not going to accept it at all and I don't want to waste my energy there. Let me come to the reason of my being here. We haven't been out for long. I think we should reunite and choose a place to go out together." Mehul was surely bored.

Frankly speaking, even I was getting bored. We all decided to meet at the canteen and discuss the plan to go out somewhere.

"Guys, only two months of our graduation are left. I think we should plan a trip which will give us memories for a lifetime," Naaz said.

"Aman, where are you taking us this time?" Nayra asked.

"I think this Sunday we should visit Lonavala," I said.

"Sunday? Who's gonna wait till Sunday?" Mehul said.

"So what, you want to go now? And it's already seven in the evening. Your favourite sunset point is closed now," Naaz said.

"But I thought the sun sets every day, without a miss," Mehul said.

"I don't want to miss classes, it's a working day. We can manage that on Saturday, I guess," Naaz said.

"See guys, I'm telling you. These sudden trips are always memorable and I want to leave right away," Mehul said.

"Cool guys, let's leave right away. We all need a break and I have a plan," Aman said. "If not sunset, what about sunrise?" Aman asked Mehul.

"I would like that, but who's going to wake up so early, man?" Mehul said. Most of us were not ready to wake up so early.

"Even I won't wake up so early. What if we do a night out? And we will be back till morning. We can attend our lectures too that way," Aman said.

After so much of discussion, we all decided to make a trip and come back to the college before the first lecture in the morning. Lonavala was not too far from our college. It would take around two hours to reach the sunrise point.

The mornings were too cold, so we took some winter wear with us. But the biggest question was the leisure time; it was just

8 p.m., so we decided to visit the night club of the city. It was Thursday, so entry for couples was free.

"Guys, we are three boys and two girls. We have to do some jugaad for me," Mehul said.

"Don't worry, Mehul. I'll be there with you," Naaz said.

"Then what about me?" I said.

"I think you are already committed," Naaz said.

"Okay guys, you all enjoy. I'm not coming," I replied as reflex.

"Dumbo! Just get inside the car. We will do something for you too," Naaz said.

"If you take Maan with you, I am not coming," Mehul said.

"Now what happened to you?" Nayra said.

"No one will remain outside the club, man. We will do something," Naaz said.

All of us got inside the car. It was already chilly and it started raining. One of the windows next to the back seat in the car couldn't be rolled up completely. I was sitting right there, and rain drops were wetting my clothes. We reached the night club in half an hour. Now all of us were thinking of ways to enter the club without paying a penny. We were observing the entry method. They were putting an ink stamp on the wrist of every person entering. Singles were holding tickets in their hands. And all that aside, Naaz was staring at my pants.

"Naaz, I haven't peed or anything. That's just rain water, so stop staring. You are embarrassing me."

"I have an idea, Maan. You will enter with me first, then Nayra and Aman will follow us," Naaz started to explain her plan.

"What about me then? You are cheating on me, Naaz. This is not done," Mehul said.

"Stop behaving like a child! I know how to take you inside, so please don't create any scene here," Naaz said.

I followed Naaz, showing my middle finger to Mehul. She allowed me to enter first and came behind me. We were stamped on our wrists. She held my hand in her and we went inside. As soon as we reached the foyer of the club she told me to wait near a particular sofa till she brought Mehul with her. I asked her about the plan and told her that they won't make a double stamp at all. In response, she showed me her wrist. To my surprise, there was nothing on her wrist.

She came near me and whispered, "Sorry, I used your wet jeans."

Before I could say anything, she turned back to get Mehul inside. She let her hair loose to change her look. I couldn't take my eyes off her. She managed to bring Mehul inside soon enough. This was a first time for all of us. In a few minutes, there was an announcement about free liquor for girls, but the condition was that they would be served directly into their mouth by a bartender. Listening to this, Nayra was in seventh heaven.

Mehul dragged me and Naaz to the dance floor. Aman and Nayra were enjoying their free drinks. The drink was free only for girls, but Nayra was filling her mouth with the free alcohol and kissing Aman. Sounds awful, right! But they were actually doing that.

Naaz was continuously staring at someone while dancing on the floor. And that someone was staring at her too. Something was burning inside me. I just wanted to stop that stare game. Even Mehul noticed that, but we preferred to stay out of it and continued dancing.

"Naaz, I don't think that guy's nice for you." I couldn't control and tried to stop Naaz from staring at the stranger.

"Let me decide that, Maan," Naaz replied.

"I'll go and have a drink." Naaz went to the bartender and had some liquor. Instead of coming back to us, she went to that guy. They started talking, but since the music was loud, they were whispering into each other's ears. I did not like it at all.

So I told Mehul to wait for me for a while and I went to Naaz. I pulled her arm and started dancing with her. She stared at me for a while and turned back to that guy for dancing. I again pulled her, but this time with force.

"You are hurting me, Maan."

"What's the problem buddy? We are dancing together," that man said.

"You stay out of this," I said looking at that guy.

"Who the hell you are? She wants to dance with me!" That guy said louder than ever. Naaz turned to him and was trying to calm him down, but before she could say anything more, I punched that guy on his face.

"What the hell Maan! Are you out of your mind? I can't believe you did that." Naaz screamed at me. Aman, Nayra, Mehul all ran up to us to handle the situation. Everything got messed up and we were thrown out of the club.

Aman was too drunk by now. The only sober person was me. So I decided to drive the car. I took the driver seat and asked everyone for the next destination.

"Buddy, shit like this happens. Let's forget it and drive to Lonavala. The sunrise is waiting for us," Aman said.

On the way, we took almost fifteen stops to pee and puke. Silence hung high in the car. Naaz was trying to sleep, but couldn't. She was in deep thoughts. Even I had a feeling of guilt. I did not have an answer for why I did what I did.

We reached the sunrise point by 5:45 p.m. Sunrise was to be close to 6:15 a.m. according to the mobile application. It was windy and cold. All my friends were mostly out of hangover now. Aman was still struggling, but was at least talking sense now. All of us came out of the car. We stood at the edge of the mountain and held each other's hand, and opened our arms to welcome the warm sun. I took a long breath and turned my head to my friends. I thanked god to have given me such brilliant friends. A tear ran down from Aman's eye. But that wasn't a sign of worry; he was still smiling. A similar smile adorned all the faces. I turned back to the sun and closed my eyes to welcome him.

The orange shade was slowly spreading all over the sky. The sounds of birds was making the scene much more alive.

"Guys, I'm freezing. Can we go inside the car?" Mehul said.

"You guys go, I'll be there in a minute," I said. All of them turned to the car, except Naaz.

"Naaz, come fast!" Mehul shouted.

"I'll be there," Naaz said.

"I'm sorry Naaz. I don't know why I behaved like that. And I think you should go back to the car. You might catch a cold."

"You don't need to worry about my cold and all. Just wanted to say that the punch was powerful, Maan. Where did you get that much energy?" We started laughing at that.

"Let's shout out our all bloody thoughts, what say?" I said. And she agreed on that. Both of us screamed our lungs out to the hills. Once done, we started laughing again and at the end we hugged each other. And I said sorry again and again.

Back in the car, Mehul sat on the driving seat, Aman and Nayra both sat on the front seat together, and we took the back seat. In a few minutes, I was sleepy. When I looked at Naaz's legs, I could see a pillow. I kept my head on her lap, and she didn't resist. I don't know when I went into a deep sleep.

After a few minutes, I heard my phone ring. It was Kiara's call. I stood straight and spoke to her. And in the end, 'same to you' came out of my mouth. I realised I wasn't comfortable during the call. Something was wrong, but what?

This was truly the most memorable trip of all times. But that incident between me and Naaz was poking at me, over and over. That again dropped me into the world of thoughts. My feelings for her were changing now. Some new feelings were showing themselves. And guess what, my group again got a new topic to discuss.

Mehul was trying to convince me that I still loved Naaz, and I should propose to her. I tried to explain that I had done all that at the night club as a friend, and nothing else.

A week had passed, and I still hadn't been able to talk to Kiara properly. Mehul wanted another trip, a longer one. But since we couldn't plan it right away, we settled for another plan.

We planned a movie night. We would watch the 11.30 p.m. show and then go to a friend's PG to stay. College gates closed at 11.00 p.m. and no students were allowed to enter the gate without prior permission after that. That plan was something new to me. We got tickets for the re-released *Titanic,* in 3D.

"Why the hell this movie guys? We have watched this a thousand times," Aman said.

"Chill yaar, all other shows are full," I said.

We went inside the theatre and took our seats. Naaz was sitting next to me. The movie started and the simple hand rest between me and Naaz became a point of notice. Naaz kept her hand on that and I was troubled to keep my hand. So I pushed her hand down and kept mine. She did the same to me. I again pushed her hand and won that place again. But this time, she didn't push my hand away. She kept her hand on mine. That gave me some goose bumps and some very wrong thoughts.

We watched the whole movie like that. I actually didn't focus as much on the movie as I focussed on her touch. I knew she felt the same, because we had rubbed our hands together at some point. But there was something stopping us.

"Guys, now what?" I asked once the movie ended.

"My friend's PG! I told you my friend lives on rent and we are going there," Aman said.

"Yeah, but I thought of going somewhere else," Mehul said and added, "See guys, we are having very less time left to spend with each other now. I don't think we would be having such leisure in future. Exams are coming, please guys…" he almost pleaded.

"I'm driving the car to my friend's room. Till then, give me a better idea. Else we will reach there," Aman started driving. We all were giving different options, but were not coming to a conclusion.

Suddenly Naaz said, "Budhwar Peth?"

A few seconds of silence prevailed and then I said, "Do you even know what that actually is?"

"It was India's largest red light area once," Naaz said. We all looked at each other. If she didn't have a problem, why should we? We all agreed to visit Budhwar Peth.

"Where the hell did you get this idea?" I asked.

"I just saw the sign board. I want to have a look," Naaz said.

"I don't think we would be able to see anything. It's already 2.30 a.m. It would be closed," Aman said.

"I don't want to see sex workers; I just want to see the area," Naaz said.

"No, actually, we were thinking of something else," Mehul mumbled.

"What did he just say?" Nayra asked suddenly.

"Nothing! Nayra, why don't you start the Google map?" I tried to cover up. We all reached the place and saw that the roads were empty. I don't know about the others, but boys for sure were looking for something specific. Our intension was not bad at all; we just wanted to see a woman of trade and how she'd look. But there was pin-drop silence, except some dogs barking. On both sides of the road, there were old buildings with very small galleries.

"Some of them must be standing right there," Naaz pointed out a place.

"I think somebody's there." I saw a car at a distance.

"Hell, that's a police car. Shall we go back?" Aman said.

"No, if we go back, they will definitely doubt us. Just go straight!" I said.

And what we were fearing happened. The policemen stopped us.

"Where are you going?" a policeman asked us.

"Sir, we had gone for a movie, and now we are going back to our hostel," Aman said.

"And who are these girls?"

"We are all friends from the same college, sir," Aman replied calmly.

"Show me your movie tickets."

"I just threw them in a dustbin outside the multiplex."

*"Chutiya banata he*? Come out!" He got angry. Aman tried to convince him, but he was not ready to accept it. "I said, come out, you fucker!" he shouted.

"Go out, Aman," I whispered and added, "Offer him something and finish it yaar." He just nodded his head and went out. The policeman took Aman with him to his jeep. We saw Aman joining his hands and begging in front of the policeman. He also took out his purse, but the policeman slapped him after looking at the purse.

"Oh shit! Let me go out," I said.

"No, I think I can handle this," Naaz said. She opened her hairclip and put on some red lipstick on her face before opening the car door.

"Naaz, I don't think you should go. If you have made up your mind, I'll come with you," I said.

"I know I can get him back. You stay here." She went out without listening to me. She adjusted her dress and went to the jeep.

She took a seat next to Aman. She started talking with the policeman. And in a few minutes, they came back. The policeman's fingerprints were clearly visible on Aman's face.

"How much did he take?" I asked. Aman took the front seat without a word and drove the car.

"Nothing!" Naaz said.

"That's not possible. Tell me what did you say to him?"

"Nothing much. I just told him Aman was lying. That Nayra and I are prostitutes from Hotel Meena. We can join him the next day for free if he wants," Naaz said.

"Does that hotel exists or not?" I asked.

"Yeah, I saw it listed on Google maps. Luckily, he believed us and even took my contact number and made a call to cross-check," she said.

"Are you out of your mind? Why did you give him your number? We might get into trouble," Nayra said.

"I gave him the wrong number, and told him to make just one ring. I also told him my phone was in the car."

"You are great. Aman, you should be thankful to Naaz," Mehul said.

"Yeah, I should be thankful to her. She brought us all here in the first place," Aman said.

"Okay, finally the problem is solved. Now, where else?" Mehul asked.

"Nowhere, I'm driving to my friend's house," Aman said.

"Okay Aman, no issues. Can you just show us your face? We just want to see those fingerprints," Mehul said. He didn't reply and kept driving quietly. I seriously did not want to laugh, but it just came out. I laughed so loud that one by one, everyone joined me.

"Stop it, guys! All this has happened just because of you guys," Aman said and after a few seconds, he joined the laughter club too.

Aman drove us to his friend's PG. It was around 3 a.m. I was observing Naaz the whole way. I was wondering if I should give a thought to Mehul's observation about us. I mean, I might really love her. But I was getting married soon, so I had to stay away from Naaz.

We were too tired so we started getting ready to sleep at the places marked out for us. Everyone found a suitable place, except me and Naaz. There was only one place left – a double bed. One place was already occupied by Mehul. So it was sure for me to take another place beside him. Now Naaz was all alone and tried to find a place. Finally she took a chair and tried to sleep on that, but it didn't work. I shifted closer to Mehul and offered her some space on the bed.

Without denying, she took the place next to me. She lay down straight, facing the fan, and closed her eyes. Even I closed my eyes and pretended to sleep, but in reality I was unable to sleep. Thoughts were bursting out like a volcano; they were making my night sleepless. I didn't even realize when I turned towards her. I could see her neck and her ears. I kept one hand on her stomach and wondered how things were happening beyond my control.

She was breathing heavily and I could sense that. I went closer to her and kissed her on her ear. Her breathing sped up. Then I went ahead and kissed her on her neck. More than anything else, she adjusted her neck in a way that I could kiss her easily. That gave me surety that she was awake and she wanted the same from me.

My fear of rejection was now reducing slowly. She turned to face me, her eyes still closed. I kissed her on her lips and she kissed me back. Then she pulled me towards her and hugged me tight. That night we did mostly everything with our clothes on. We just didn't cross the limit.

I just held her hand in mine and went into a deep sleep with a smile on my face. Most of the things were clear in my mind now. The next morning was going to be more beautiful.

We all woke up in a few hours. All of us got ready and went back to the hostel. Naaz and I couldn't get much time to talk. I went to my room and was getting ready for the class when Mehul came to my room to catch up.

"Maan, today you have to look more special, so take your time."

"I don't understand, Mehul?"

He closed the door of my room and said, "I know what happened last night."

I got nervous now, but I behaved like nothing had happened. It wasn't working, so I yelled at him and tried to convince him, "What the hell, who told you about this? I mean how did you know? I mean I didn't want to do that, you understand, right?"

"Calm down, my boy! I was awake… actually I was not awake, but your movements woke me up. And don't worry, your secret is safe with me."

"Thank you yaar, but now what? I am too tensed," I asked him.

"What do you mean what now? Maan, make it clear to yourself that you love Naaz. Why do you keep denying it?"

"I still don't know about loving her. Maybe it was just an accident."

"I don't understand what you want, Maan."

"Mehul, I'm not denying my feelings, but you know that I'm getting married. I should not be with Naaz. Even if I have feelings for Naaz, I have to hide them, because it's too late."

"It's not late, not yet. You are not married yet. Just talk to Kiara."

"Mehul, Kiara is a really nice girl. I just can't say no to her."

"Okay then, give me your phone… I'll do that for you."

"No! If it comes to telling her, I will tell her myself. I don't need your help."

"Okay than, call her now. I am waiting outside."

"Now? Are you mad? We are getting late for class."

"Now means now…you are calling her now." Without listening to me, he went outside and locked the door from outside.

"Now you can come out only when you are finished with her," he shouted from the outside.

"Is there any girl inside?" I could hear someone asking Mehul.

"Yes, please save her from me… Open the door buddy!" I shouted from inside.

"Just go and do your own work," Mehul said to him.

"Hey listen, could you arrange someone for me too?" he asked Mehul.

"Let Maan finish it first, then she will come to you. Now just go and wait in your room," I heard Mehul say.

"Yaar please Mehul, open the door!"

"I can't hear you till you make that call."

I was sure that Mehul was not going to open the door. I had to make a call. I picked up the phone from my bed and dialled Kiara. My heartbeats were rising and I couldn't take it. I disconnected the phone.

"Buddy, I can't do this, and I'm not even attending the lecture. You go ahead!"

"Okay, I don't mind. Let Naaz sit with another guy in class, and that Rafiq is always finding an opportunity to impress Naaz anyway. Don't you think Rafiq looks better than you? Even I think so," Mehul was trying to make me feel jealous and strangely, that was working.

"Don't try to make me feel jealous; this won't work on me. But just because you are insisting, I'm calling Kiara, okay?"

"Hello, Kiara… yeah hi!" I called her up.

"Hi Maan, I think you should be in your lecture now right. Anything wrong?"

"Nothing's wrong Kiara, I think everything's going to be right now. I just wanted to say that I'm sorry." I told Kiara everything about me and Naaz. She didn't say a word till the end, when I stopped talking. The feelings which I was going through were horrible.

After a pause that held me on the edge, she said, "Maan, I'm glad you shared these things with me. I am so happy that you trusted me enough. Maan, I just want to tell you that I have loved you more than anybody in my life, and can't forget you. If at any time you change your mind, just don't hesitate to call me. I'll always be there, waiting for you."

I was surprised at how clear she was about herself. Those sentences made it clear that she was a pure-hearted girl.

"You know Kiara, you will be my best friend. I feel horrible at doing this, but I didn't want to lie to you. I'll make sure that you get someone better than me, someone who truly deserves you."

"Leave all that side. First you go and propose to Naaz. Best of luck, Maan," she said softly.

"I love you Kiara, and thank you for understanding me."

"Don't use those words for me. Save them for Naaz. Bye!"

Before I could say bye, she had hung up. I could imagine the pain she was going through and that was all because of me. Truly she was a gem of a person and I had broken her heart. Mehul had overheard everything and was happy that I had cleared it out with Kiara. He opened the door and hugged me.

"I am too happy for you, brother," Mehul told me. We left for the class.

Naaz was already in class, but I was too nervous to say anything to her. I just went and took a seat next to her and said "Hi".

She replied with a hi, but that excitement was missing. Usually we talked a lot in class. But today, it was different. It seemed she was not comfortable with me at all. She was behaving like we were meeting for the first time. I felt like I was talking to some stranger. I decided to talk to her during the break. After the first lecture, I turned to face her but before I could say anything, she had gone out of the classroom. I followed her. I wanted to clear out everything, but her behaviour was making me feel guilty, like I had done something wrong to her, something she did not want to be a part of.

I needed to know the reason behind such a behaviour. I walked up to her to clear out things, but before I could say anything, she looked at me and said, "Hey Maan, I just want to have some alone time, if you don't mind."

I didn't say a word to her, but instead of going back to class, I went to my room. Mehul tried to stop me, but I was seething with anger. I pushed him back and went directly to my room. Mehul followed me with our bags in his hands. I locked the door from inside before he could walk in.

"Open the door, Maan! What happened to you?" Mehul was knocking at the door and shouting from outside.

"Fuck you man, I told you she doesn't love me. I was right, Mehul! Why the hell did you drive me to her?" I screamed from inside.

"Maan, please first open the door, we will talk inside," Mehul requested me. I was too weak to handle myself. I opened the door and hugged him. "Mehul she doesn't love me at all."

"Maan, listen to me, and look at me… there's nothing like that. I know her. She loves you more than anything."

"No, that's not true. She is not interested in even talking to me."

"Oh Maan, so you haven't even talked to her? How can you be so judgmental? Maybe she needs some time to accept things, nothing else."

"Mehul, she was looking at me like I have done something wrong to her, but that's not true. Both of us were equally involved."

"Can you please forget what happened today and give it another try? Just go and talk to her!"

"No, Maan. I don't think I will be able to do that. I don't have the courage to hear a 'no' from her." I was totally broken.

I had expected something else from her. And everything that was happening was the absolute opposite. Mehul was trying to make the situation better, though.

We both decided to avoid that topic for a while. We decided to be normal, like nothing had happened. I was not ready to lose her friendship, so I made up my mind to not propose to her and just behave normally. I decided not to meet her the whole day. I kept myself busy with books. In the evening, I was looking outside the window and was in deep thought when my phone rang. It was Kiara.

"Sorry, I might be disturbing you both Maan, but I was just curious to know her reaction," she said.

"Kiara, I haven't said anything yet."

"Oh! Why are you sounding so low?"

"Nothing like that… it was a hard day, so I'm a bit tired."

"I'm sure Naaz won't deny your proposal, you have something special in you."

"Thank you, Kiara." I was talking to her and was continuously getting someone's call. I looked at the phone screen and saw Naaz's name flashing.

"Kiara, can we talk later? Someone's call is waiting."

"Yeah bye, and don't forget that I'm waiting for the good news." Without replying to her, I dropped the call and called up Naaz.

"Duffer, where are you?" Naaz was shouting on the other side. This was her usual self. This change in her behaviour was making me comfortable and relaxed.

"Nothing Naaz, I was feeling a bit low," I told her.

"Come to my room and collect your notes."

"What? At your room? Are you mad?"

"What's to be mad in that? You are allowed to enter the girls' hostel till 7.00 p.m. And it's only 6. You were not in class so I thought you will need my notes."

I don't understand Naaz at all sometimes. Yesterday night, she was different; today morning, she was strange, and now she was just being weird. Without wasting a minute, I ran to the girls' hostel. There was a lady standing outside the gate. She had a register book for entry and exit. I was hesitating to talk to her, but the excitement of meeting Naaz made me stronger.

"So, where do you want to go?" the lady asked me.

"I have written everything in the register, you can read that. I think I'm allowed to enter the hostel without prior permission of anyone," I said with an attitude.

I ran towards the lift. A few girls were already waiting for the lift and that was an awkward moment. They looked at me like I had come to visit the hostel to molest someone. My reactions went blank after a while. I pressed the fourth floor button. The girls standing behind me were fighting to see which floor I had pressed. I reached the floor, and went straight to see the floor map. The girls were interested to know where I was going, so they didn't press the door closing button. I waited for the lift doors to close and then ran towards room no. 418. The room was open. I entered the room and closed the door.

"What happened?" Naaz asked.

"What happened? Look at way the other girls were looking at me. Like, I have come here with a crime in mind or something," I said with heavy breath.

"Just ignore them, they will talk for a day or two and then forget about it. You have a cup of coffee."

"Thank god you are not like that, or I would have never been your friend."

"By the way, Maan, I wanted to call you long ago, but did not have the courage. When I gathered the guts to call you, you were busy. Actually, it was not only notes. I wanted to tell you something else."

I crossed my fingers as she stood up and went to her study table, and started fidgeting with her computer.

"I'm here now, you can tell me."

"Nothing much. I just wanted to say that some things happen in life, and we should just move ahead of those… Whatever happened between us was just a mistake, I think," she said and kept looking into the computer screen.

"Actually, you are right. Even I thought we should forget about it. But I'm happy that you at least initiated the topic," I said.

"Thank you for understanding me, Maan." She continued doing some stuff on her computer and then said, "Maan, I'm having some problem with this computer. I don't know why, but it hangs many times in a day." I noticed she was trying hard to reconnect.

"Let me check." I went to the PC and tried to check what the problem was. "I think there's a virus in your PC. Let me just restart." I said and pressed the button for restarting the computer. My breath fell on her ears. And she was turning again and again to talk with me. Our eyes started playing games and at one point, they could not move away and froze.

I tucked a free strand of her hair behind her ear. I leaned in and kissed her on her cheek.

"Please, control Maan." Her words were not saying what her body language indicated. She suddenly stood up from her chair and turned towards me. She caught my hand and took me to her bed. She gave me a hard kiss and almost threw me on her bed.

Things were going out of control pretty fast when her dad started calling. She disconnected the phone and started kissing me again. A few deep kisses later, she stopped and went back to her chair.

"What happened, Naaz?" I asked her

"Can you please leave the room now?" She was crying, but I couldn't say anything at that point. I directly went to Mehul's room and told him what had happened.

"Yaar, I totally don't understand this girl, but I think I should talk to her."

"Do whatever you want to do Mehul, but now I am fed up with this," I said with anger and dropped down on the bed.

A week had passed. I had told Kiara that Naaz had accepted my proposal, so she hadn't been calling since last week. Aman and Nayra had no clue about all this and planned an ice cream trip on Monday night. I was not interested at all but Aman forced me to come. I think the same happened with Naaz too.

Aman and Nayra took front seats as usual. Mehul took the window seat at the back knowingly. Naaz and I had no option but to sit together. Except me and Naaz, everyone was talking. I was not even listening to anything. We reached the destination a few minutes later. Nayra and Aman were going to order ice creams.

I went with Aman and Nayra to help them but the line was too long and they told me to go back. I went back and saw Mehul and Naaz talking. 'They might be talking about me,' I thought. So I stood behind a tree, from where I could hear them properly without being seen.

"Naaz, he loves you a lot and you can't even imagine how much he cares about you," Mehul said.

"Oh, so he has sent you to propose to me? Don't you feel shameful in asking me that?" Naaz screamed at Mehul.

"I'm not asking anything, I'm just sharing this with you. And let me make it clear that nobody has sent me here. It was my own decision to talk to you."

"Okay than, I would like you to share one thing with Maan. Tell him to stop dreaming about me. I am a Muslim girl and I don't want to be in touch with him anymore. He is so senseless. Tell him that I don't love him and I won't even think about it in my dreams."

I couldn't hear more disgusting words for me, so I left the place. I never understood why she was doing all that. I went back to my room on my own. Honestly, I didn't know what I was supposed to do next. On the one hand, it was clear that Naaz did not have feelings for me. On other hand, I was hoping to get attached with her. The only thing I could think of in this situation was to call Kiara.

"Hi Maan. It's been so long. How's Naaz, by the way?" she asked.

"I want to get married to you, Kiara." I told her without further ado.

"Maan, are you okay? I hope you know who you have called. I'm Kiara, not Naaz," she said in a breaking voice.

"I know it's you Kiara. But I'm tired now."

"Tired of what, Maan? Every relationship goes through ups and downs, but that doesn't mean you should break up with her. It has just been a week or two of you proposing to her. Give some time to your relationship."

"Time to a relationship? What relationship are you talking about? I never proposed her, Kiara. Her body language tells me that she hates me."

I started crying like a child and added, "You know Kiara, my father was right. He always told me that nothing like love exist… it's just a physical attraction you feel. And those two or three nights don't mean I love her at all, and I have to accept that."

"Maan, listen to me first. I would suggest you to go and talk to her first, tell her about your feelings, tell her how much you love her, and then you can make a decision."

"I heard everything she told Mehul, and now I can't go there and insult my feelings. She clearly said that she doesn't love me. I think Dad was right; I thought this was love, but it wasn't. It can't be. Kiara, I promise that I will come out of it and will keep you happy all your life."

"I know you by heart. You can't harm anyone, and I know how much you respect women, I have already told you that whenever you feel right, you can come back into my life, and I will welcome you with open arms. Another thing I hadn't told you earlier, but I had decided to never get married."

"What? Why did you take such a decision?"

"You are the reason, Maan. I love you a lot and can't think about anyone else now. See, at any point of time, you can go back to Naaz if that makes you happy, because your happiness is my priority."

"Why are you so good, Kiara? Don't be this nice, you might get hurt someday."

"When you are there, I don't need to be worried."

"Kiara, my final exams will end next week. After that, I'll be back home and I want to get married next month. Are you ready for that?"

"I'm ready for marrying you even today, but what about you? Are you ready, Maan?"

"Yes, I'm ready, and now my decision won't change. I think I would be the luckiest man in the world to have a wife like you. I might need some time to come out of things, but I'm sure I'll be very happy with you."

"Thank you for understanding me and having faith in me."

This conversation with Kiara helped me make up my mind and come to a decision. I thought my decision was right and I was very lucky to have a girl like Kiara. With Naaz, I thought it was just physical attraction and I could just be friends with her. She was right about forgetting everything and remaining friends. Just one thought was killing me at that time – Would it be easy to be just friends with a girl I had felt so strongly about?

Some things are very messy in life. You try hard, but you are not able to understand what is happening around you. I made up my mind to get married to Kiara and even she agreed on that. But now the last few days of my college were going to be the toughest days of my life.

❖

All of us were busy preparing for the exams. I was not thinking about anything else and it was a welcome distraction from the confusion. I was trying to focus on my studies. Those days, Naaz and I hardly met with a few greetings. Things were getting normal between us, though. I had accepted her as a friend.

By the time the exams got over, it felt like a huge achievement. Plus, I had already spread the news about my marriage to my friends, even Naaz knew about it. It was the last day of college, after which we all were heading back home. I still remember that day. And I regret that I couldn't do what I should have done that day.

I was done with my packing and was feeling hungry, so I went directly to the canteen. While coming back from the canteen, a girls' hostel warden called out to me.

"Hey boy, come here!"

"Yes ma'am," I waited for her order.

"Can you please help us in getting out some luggage of these girls? Geeta will help you in that." She asked me for help. I nodded and followed Geeta. We took the lift and she pressed the fourth floor button.

"You take the luggage from this room, I'll collect from another one. Also, see if she needs some help in packing, please. But behave well. You are in a girls' hostel," she said.

"Okay, Geeta ji."

God wanted this, I think. It was Naaz's room. I knocked at the door and a voice came from inside.

"Geeta, come inside! I'll just take a few minutes." I went inside her room; it was all clear she was just taking some stuff from inside and her eyes were fixed inside the cupboard. Maybe she was packing the last few things or something.

"Take this and keep it in the yellow bag," she said, handing over her innerwear, without looking back.

"It's me, Naaz," I replied her with awkwardness. She took a sudden turn and her hands went behind her with lightning speed to hide her clothes.

"I'm sorry. I should have told you before entering the room," I said.

"What are you doing here? I mean, even you have to pack."

"Your warden called me here to help some girls take their luggage downstairs. So, do you need any help or…?"

"Actually everything's done. Just one thing, which is in my hands. I think I should do that by myself and after that, you can be the coolie for me."

"You are cheap, you know that!" She went near to her bag on the bed. She turned back to me once she had zipped the bag up.

"Now we won't be able to meet so often, Maan. Days are going to be tough for me now. Time flies! Thank you for being my best friend," she said, teary-eyed.

"Oh my god, look at you! I have never heard you so low and I think you'll make me cry. You know what Naaz, even I won't forget you," I told her. I saw some red coloured thread on her T-shirt and wanted to remove it. So I went near her and drove my hand towards her stomach to remove that thread. She opened her arms a bit, but I couldn't understand why.

"It was a thread," I said, handing it over to her. She pulled her arms back down. And then I realized that she wanted a hug from me. I needed one too. I still remember and regret till date that I couldn't hug her that day. Even today, I think if I could travel in time, I'd go back and hug her tight. I was not sure whether we would be able to meet later or not.

"Naaz, I want to say something to you." I dared.

"Yeah say!" We were looking at each other.

"But I'm afraid that I might even loose our friendship," I said.

"Then don't say it. I don't want to lose your friendship." There was a pause for a few seconds.

"So, you are coming for the marriage, right?" I tried to break the awkward silence.

"Maan, I would love to attend your marriage, but you know I have been placed in a multinational company already. I don't think I should take leave in the very first month of my job for your marriage."

"I do understand. I think you are right. We can meet afterwards," I told her.

This was our last conversation before I took her luggage downstairs. Her parents were already waiting outside. Most of the students were very emotional. I wanted to hug Naaz and cry for some time, but I couldn't do that because of the awkwardness and anxiety left over from the past few incidents. We both couldn't help it that day.

After saying goodbye, I went back to my room to pick up my stuff. I was the last one to leave the hostel among the group of five. I took my luggage and went out of the college. I tried hard to not cry, but couldn't stop. I just went to the stone in front of our college gate and sat on it. I looked at the college for a few minutes and cried a lot. A gatekeeper came to me and kept his hand on my shoulder and said, "In the last so many years, I have never seen a guy like you. You are too attached to the college or maybe with someone. Just keep the memories with you in your heart and go ahead in your life. This was just a part of your life. Be strong, there's so much to come yet. Just cry everything out so that you can be stronger and move on as a better person."

"I couldn't even meet her properly, and I had dreamt a lot about us. I don't even know whether she loves me or not." I could not control myself and burst out. In that moment, I was not sure if my decision to marry Kiara was right or wrong.

"Just go and talk to her; everything will be solved," he said. I didn't reply and just took my luggage with me and walked away.

# 6

# When Actual Life Began

"Why is everyone taking so much time? And you, I had told you a thousand times to keep this vase over there. No one is listening to me. I don't know how much I can work."

My dad was shouting at every one. He was too happy that his son was getting married. He just wanted to make sure everything was perfect.

"Dad, just calm down! Everything will be fine."

"My dear son, you won't understand this yet. You are my only son, and I want you to get married like a prince. So, no interference, please."

"I know Dad, you are not going to rest at all till I get married, but I just want you to give me some work or to others. Don't take everything on yourself, let me help you . Why are you not letting me help?"

"Are you mad? Your Mom will kill me if I give you any work. Our rituals say that the groom should not work in his own marriage, and you don't worry. I'll handle everything. Look over there, your friends are here! Just go and welcome them." Dad is a superhero for me and he was hell bent on proving it too.

Aman, Nayra and Mehul had just come and all of them had changed so much. Nayra wore a sari and Aman was holding her. They were the first ones to get married among us.

"So, finally you are getting married! I remember you were going to get married just after a month of our college. But I'm happy you changed your decision," Nayra said.

"Dude, I think you should not get married at all. Try to be in a live-in instead; that might make you clear about your partner. You can find some secrets too," Aman said.

Nayra looked at Aman and said with a fierce expression, "So, you have found some secrets about me? Please explain, dear husband," Nayra said.

"Nothing much, I just came to know that you wake up at midnight and do some unusual stuff," Aman said.

"What kind of stuff?" I asked, enjoying their friendly banter.

"A few days back, she was laughing in the middle of the night, sitting on the bed," Aman said and chuckled.

"God, we had a great day, and I was dreaming about it. And it's okay to laugh at night, I guess," Nayra said in defence. I agreed on that, so that she didn't feel cornered.

"That might be normal, but what about a slap? You remember that, right?" Aman turned to Nayra. "Maan, you won't believe that she literally slapped me at midnight when I was in deep sleep. Just imagine the scenario! And her laughter is no better than a horror show," Aman spilled the beans.

"Yaar, these two will not finish with their fights; they are the same as they were in college. Tell me, where's Naaz?" Mehul asked.

"She must be getting ready," I said.

"I think I should help her," Nayra said and left to meet Naaz.

"I think we should go to my room. We are blocking everyone's way. And you guys can help me get ready. Guests have started coming, and I can't look like this," I said and took everyone upstairs. Naaz was stuck somewhere in my head and her thoughts were leading me to my room. How she would look today. It was a special day; and I wanted her to look special.

"Don't you think your room is too small? You can't do stuff here… I mean, it's your first night," Aman said.

"Buddy, I do have a bed and that's enough for me," I said.

"No, but I think a sofa works better, and even a chair. Like this, you know," Aman was explaining with gestures.

"I'll think about it later. You go and get Nayra. What is taking her so long?" I said.

"Brother, stop taking stress and take my advice; you'll be happy for a lifetime. You need to lubricate your engine well to get a powerful performance. And in that powerful performance, you can add some stars by trying different locations, Just drive safely." He kept on speaking until he was pushed out of the room.

"Now you are looking great, just put this stole in this way." Mehul arranged the stole in a particular way. Meanwhile, I heard Nayra, Aman and Naaz coming. Naaz was standing behind Aman and Nayra at the door. I was able to see only her face. So calm and bright she looked. Aman and Nayra entered the room and now Naaz was clearly visible to me. I remembered the first day of college when I had seen her. She was carrying the same look even today. Just the colour of the dress was different.

"Oh my god, look at you! Kiara won't be able to take her eyes off you," Naaz said to me.

"Thanks a lot, Naaz. You aren't looking too bad either," I said.

"Bad? My foot! It's my best friend's wedding, how can I look bad!" Naaz said.

"Obviously, you might have got help from Kiara, otherwise…" I stopped my sentence in between.

"So, you mean I did not look good when I was in college?" Naaz said.

"Guys, we exist! And Naaz, we have arrived today. You might have chatted with him yesterday, but we haven't," Mehul targeted me and Naaz.

"Oh, I know about others, but thanks for informing me that even you do exist. By the way, why are you so jealous?" Naaz said.

"Guys, we should bring Kiara here and should have some selfies, what say?" Nayra asked everyone with excitement.

"I think you are right. Mehul, you stay here with Maan; we will go and get Kiara here," Aman said.

"Guys, she might not be ready yet," I said.

"That we will figure out, you don't need to be worried," Naaz said.

"Okay, now I don't want to say anything, you guys go and do your stuff." I did not want to argue with them. They went outside the room to get Kiara. I could not stop myself from looking at Naaz. She turned back and smiled at me from the door.

"She's gone now, Maan. Please come out of your dreams." Mehul dragged me out of my thoughts.

"Yeah, I know they are gone, so what's up nowadays? How's your job and all? Going good?" I was trying to change the topic.

"You still love her, right?"

"Are you mad? Naaz is just my friend, we have moved on now."

"I didn't take her name, Maan."

"I know that, but I know you were asking about her. I don't want to talk about that at all now. I hope you understand."

"No, I don't understand Maan. Why are you doing this to yourself? This is literally a suicide." His voice was getting louder.

"Calm down! Somebody will hear you."

"Oh, if you don't love her, why do you even care about others. Others will think I'm a fool. Why you are so worried?" Mehul was being unusual.

"Just stop thinking about me, Mehul. It's my life; let me live it in my way. You are telling me I should be with Naaz and not Kiara. You know everything, don't you!"

"Have you even tried to talk to her? Have you ever shared your feelings with her?"

"Mehul, you know that she doesn't love me at all."

"That's not my answer. Have you ever asked her?"

"You know what, Mehul! Delay in my marriage is not due to my grandfather's death. I had decided to postpone the date before he died. I wanted to give a chance to myself." I screamed at him and closed the door before adding, "The whole year, I haven't talked to Kiara as much as I have chatted with Naaz. I don't remember a single day when I didn't talk to Naaz. Those feelings just came back, Mehul. And I even expressed my feelings to her."

"What was her response?"

"She said she does not want to talk on that topic again and after that she stopped chatting with me. I felt like I had done something wrong. I was crying all alone. I was helpless. Why was she denying her love for me? I tried to not talk to her, but after a week, she again sent me a message. I don't understand what she wants."

"You still talk to her every day?"

"Yes, I do, but general talk."

"General talk, okay? Ten minutes, five or less than that?" Mehul asked me in a different tone.

"Maybe half an hour or sometimes an hour. But we don't talk about love and all; it's just daily routine we talk about." I tried to explain.

"So, you think you will stop talking to Naaz after marriage, and you will be happy with Kiara?"

"Yeah, I think. I mean I'll slow down talking to Naaz gradually and then finally a day will come when I'll stop talking to her on daily basis. But at least we will be friends."

"You don't even know what you are saying. Do you think it's that easy, Maan?"

"No, It's not going to be easy at all, and not only that, but I don't even know whether I would be able to love Kiara or not."

"Then why are you getting married to Kiara?"

"Kiara loves me more than I love Naaz. I know what pain you have to go through when your loved one does not accept you, and I have promised Kiara to keep her happy. Don't worry, she will never know that I'm unhappy or what I feel for Naaz. And who knows, one day I might fall for her too."

"Don't you think you are ruining your and Kiara's life?"

"Put yourself in my shoes and then talk," I said aggressively.

"Whatever you are doing is wrong." As soon as Mehul finished his sentence, my friends entered with Kiara. I turned to wipe off my tears and brought on a big, fake smile on my face. God has given us the great gift of facial expression. You can hide things from anyone. Just keep feelings deep inside you and bring a big smile on your face. No one will ever know what's going on inside you. They all came closer and Kiara took the place next to me. Mehul was taking some selfies. I tried hard to keep a smile on my face. I even tried hard not to cry, but despite that, a drop of tear came flowing down.

"I have to use the washroom," I said and hurried to the washroom.

"What yaar, Maan! It was going so good, and you ruined everything. Just come back soon!" Nayra was shouting at me.

"Let him freshen up. We will take pics after he comes out," Mehul said. Hopefully no one saw me crying. I just went inside the bathroom and started washing my face. I couldn't stop crying. I kept both my hands on the basin and let my feelings flow for a minute or so.

"Maan, come on yaar! Make it fast," Nayra shouted from outside.

"Just a minute." I managed to say. I washed my face again and flushed the toilet on my way out. This time I went out with a bigger smile and took pics with them.

"Maan, come! Pandit ji is calling you." Mom came inside and told me "Oh! So you are with your friends. I think you should introduce me. I know Naaz because she's here from last night," Mom said excited. I introduced her to the others.

"Guys, it was great meeting you. Your bonding is visible. Never let your friendship fade. Thank you very much for coming here," Mom said.

"Aunty, I want to ask you something?" Aman said.

"Yes, please."

"Who is younger, you or Maan?" Aman asked.

We all smiled, while Mom said, "You are asking such a silly question. Just look at my figure, my energy, and look at your friend! I might be older in age, but it's just a number. I am quite young at heart." Mom maintains herself in a better way than I could even think. "Pandit ji will kill me if you guys don't take your friend downstairs soon. Please make it quick. And Naaz, please help Kiara get ready, because Pandit ji will call her soon too."

My friends took me downstairs where Pandit ji started chanting mantras. People do get excited and also get a bit nervous when they are getting married. But here the scenario was different. I was not sure what I was doing with myself. Whether it was right or wrong, should I leave the place now. I was confused. In a few minutes, Pandit ji asked Mom to call Kiara to the mandap. Mom told Nayra to go and get her. Some music started at the bride's entry. She stood there, looking so beautiful. People around her were dancing. Naaz was looking really pretty. She was holding Kiara and was bringing her to me. At every few seconds, Naaz was flicking her hair back. A continuous smile on her face was adding more charm to it. Her long earrings were bouncing with her steps.

"Stop looking at her like this Jiju. Tonight Kiara is all yours." Someone from behind broke my concentration and reminded me that I was looking at someone else, not Kiara. I remembered my father's words, that there's nothing like love. It's just attraction and everyone goes through this phase. But now I was getting married, and such thoughts were disturbing me.

More so, Naaz was not interested in me at all and she had made it clear so many times. Still, something was wrong. I didn't realize when Kiara took her place next to me. And Naaz, where was she? My eyes were searching for her. I could not get up from my seat, so I asked Mehul to find where she was.

I waited for Mehul to come with Naaz as Pandit ji carried on with the rituals, but even he was not visible. My curiosity was at its peak and I was hoping for the best. Nothing wrong should happen to her.

Suddenly my eyes went on the screen which was playing my last night's dance performance. I was suddenly taken back in time.

"You and dance! I don't believe at all," Naaz said when we were sitting on the terrace.

"In college I was not able to dance, but I'm practicing for the last two months. I'm sure I would be doing better then you now," I said.

"I still don't believe it," she said.

"Okay, how can I make you believe? Wait a minute. I think you should ask my mom."

"Mumma's boy!" she said.

"What did you just say?"

"Nothing, I said mumma's boy. Why should I ask your mom? You should show me some moves and prove that you can dance."

"It's 6 a.m., and you brought me directly from the station to the terrace."

"My train made it earlier; that's not my fault at all. And if you want to make excuses, go ahead. It'll confirm that you can't dance."

"Idiot, there are still too many guests who are sleeping. I don't think we would be able to play any kind of music here," I gave another excuse.

"I do have a phone. I think you can play songs on this."

"And what about my partner? Kiara is not here. And I don't think couple dance can be performed all alone."

"When the world's best dancer is here with you, why are you worried?" She offered her hand to me.

"Okay, let's see if you can match up with my moves or not." I accepted her idea and played a song from her phone. Somewhere I fell, and somewhere she fell. After a few trials, we managed to get perfect steps. We were in each other's arms, away from this world.

"Oh my god, I didn't even know my son could dance so well." Mom brought us both out from our dream world.

"Yes aunty, your son has become such a great dancer. I do admit. Maan, you were right," Naaz told us.

"By the way, who are you? And what are you doing on my terrace with my son?" Mom asked quite defensively.

"Mom, she is my college friend, Naaz. I told you about her, remember? I picked her up from the station and she needed some fresh air, so we came to the terrace," I said it all before Naaz could say something.

"Beta, Pandit ji is asking you to fill *sindur* on her forehead." Mom broke my thoughts. She handed me a one-rupee coin, which had some vermilion on it. I was again confused what should I do. Will everything be fine? Because after this, I had to stop thinking about Naaz. My priority should be Kiara. My dad had always said that everything settles down with time. And even I don't know what exactly love is. I pepped myself up with those thoughts and poured that sindur to Kiara's forehead. Now I was married to Kiara.

"She's gone Maan, she had a train to catch." Mehul came and told me. I literally don't understand this girl. Why does she always behave like a jerk. She didn't even say goodbye. I wanted her to stay for longer. I couldn't call her in between the ceremony, even when I wasn't mentally involved in it.

From the next day onwards, my life was going to change. You never know what god has planned for you. Life keeps on giving surprises. Naaz was that kind of surprise for me. I couldn't have known her role in my life. Why are we not just good friends? I was not able to maintain just a good friendship with her; some little spark was always there. Some hesitation was always there. We were not as close now as when we had planted the bomb in our college. I'll never forget those beautiful days of my life. They will always be somewhere deep in my memories. That was my secret and only Mehul knew about it.

The *bidai* time is the toughest time for every girl. Not only tough for girls, but for the guys as well. They don't know how to react or what to do when the *bidai* is happening. A girl has to leave her house which holds in it all her memories – the fights with siblings, not listening to their mother, the house rules they have broken, and leaving every girl's best friend, her dad. I don't know how they manage to leave everything behind to start life afresh.

Let's think the opposite for once. What if guys were supposed to leave their house? I wouldn't be able to do that. Leaving my mom, my dad, my sibling, everyone.

Once we were inside the car, I noticed Kiara was crying a lot. I remember she was holding her dad's hand and did not want him to let go. And her father could not say a single word and was just wiping off her tears.

In life, there are some situations where you have to take some kind of decisions that are really painful. And every dad dreams about this painful moment, I think. I don't know if my decision of getting married to Kiara was right or not. If my decision of leaving Naaz was right or wrong. I was not sure about any of this. The things happening around me were no less than a drama. I was still thinking about Naaz. I still remember her last look and her smile when she was bringing Kiara to me.

Wait a minute! I think Naaz loves me and she couldn't bear to see me getting married to someone else. No, that can't be true. Then why didn't she meet me before leaving? Oh god, I miss her badly.

The driver started driving away from Kiara's dad slowly. Kiara's dad left go of her hand and folded his hands, looking at me. His gesture was clearly showing that he was requesting me to keep her daughter happy. I joined my hands too and conveyed through my eyes that he need not worry, I'm here for them.

Inside the car, Kiara had nobody around her, except me, and she was crying. I held her hand and brought her close to me. She literally broke down and I let her cry. She hugged me tightly and even my eyes were moist.

"Promise me Maan, you'll be always there for me," Kiara said in her broken voice.

"Don't worry, Kiara. I'll always be there for you, and you are now my responsibility. I promise I'll always keep you happy," I said.

I don't know why we have to trust a person so much. These arranged marriages are always like a blind game. And why only arrange marriage? In India, even love marriages are like that.

You know a person on the basis of what you see. But you don't know their daily routine, their family and several other things. I mean, you can know someone so deeply only by living with them. You can say that I'm in favour of live-in relationships for that reason. You can know them and their families thoroughly that way. After all, in India, you are not getting married to a person, but to a family.

Our car took us home. I helped her out of the car. Mom was already waiting for us with a *puja thali* in her hands. We both looked at our house, and held each other's hand as we entered. We hoped for happiness for a lifetime.

# 7

# The Addiction

When you are addicted to something and you don't get it, you try to search for an alternate. In my case, Naaz had become an addiction. Even I don't know when this happened. I had made up my mind that it was just attraction and nothing else. But I was wrong. And now, it was too late to even think about it. To get rid of that addiction, I went to others. I was in search of the same kind of conversations, the same kind of happiness, the same kind of satisfaction and the same kind of friendship which I had with Naaz.

I tried, but no one was as good as her. She was there, deep in my heart, and she had occupied so much space in my heart that there was no place for anyone else, not even Kiara.

After one year of being married, I had realised that Kiara was a gem of a person. I always tried to keep her happy and I think I succeed too. Over the years, I came to realise that my dad's theory of 'nothing like love exists' was wrong. It was his theory. I don't know what made him believe in it. I never opposed him, because it was not his fault. It was my fault that I had believed in his theory.

Over the past year, I had realised that love was life. You can live without anything, but not love. Naaz had become necessary for me to live. Days were becoming difficult for me now – fake smiles, fake happiness were taking a toll on me. But I was trying to make sure that Kiara was getting all the happiness she deserved.

"Maan, your phone is ringing; it's your colleague Jiah." I had just finished bathing when Kiara handed over my phone to me.

"Hello, yes Jiah? Just hold on for a sec." I took a shirt and gave the phone to Kiara, requesting her to put it on speaker.

"Sir, I called to remind you about the meeting at 8.00," Jiah said.

"I haven't forgotten about it, I'll be there on time. Thanks for the call," I said before hanging up.

"Kiara, please help me. Can you hand over my bag, I'm getting late," I said. She managed to give me everything, taking extra care to double check that I hadn't forgotten anything. She had prepared a delicious breakfast already.

"Kiara, your food is the best food in the whole world. But I won't be able to have it today, so just keep that for evening," I said in a hurry.

"Don't worry, just make sure you do well in the meeting. I'll make this fresh for you in the evening."

I gave her a goodbye kiss and went to my car. Ten minutes later, I was at the venue for the meeting. I took the lift up to the fifth floor and went straight into house number 505, as the door was open.

"Thank god you are on time. I think we should finish it quickly, or boss will kill us," Jiah was waiting for me.

Sometimes we travelled to work together. We used to meet up regularly, for physical gratification. Sex, actually. We both knew it was just physical and we were not mentally involved. We used to refer to it as a meeting. And I had kept the phone on speaker so that my wife didn't doubt me. Putting the phone on speaker was also our code word to signal that someone was around.

Jiah was five years older than me. According to her qualification, she was junior at work, but in experience, she was great. Let me confess, Jiah wasn't the first one I was involved with. There were two more colleagues from earlier jobs. I had changed my job thrice in one year, because every time I got intimate with a colleague, I used to change my job, to get rid of this bad habit. But god had planned something else for me. He always sent some Menaka to my life. So, I kept changing my jobs to avoid them. Not only me, but my friend Sameer had also been changing jobs with me. We had become best friends ever since my first job.

Sameer knew everything about me, about Naaz, Kiara, Jiah, and all other girls I had slept with.

"So, how was it?" Sameer asked me.

"What?" I behaved like nothing had happened today.

"Okay, fine you don't want to share. I know you regret a lot about things you don't want to do but end up doing," Sameer said.

"You know Sameer, sometimes you talk nonsense." Every time I had sex with anyone other than my wife, I used to be really furious. And he was the one who would calm me down.

"I know you are angry now, and your whole day is going to be like this. So, I won't discuss much about you and Jiah. But I would like to tell you that we have a real meeting today. Boss has called out a surprise meeting in a few minutes," he said.

"Hey kiddo! Just don't try to act smart with me. Plus, find someone for yourself, or you'll die a virgin. Look at your age!" I said.

"Ya buddy, I'm not as lucky as you are. Wife, girlfriends and..." he stopped.

"And what?"

"You know, you have told me a thousand times that you and Jiah are just friends. I don't know what to name a relationship where you indulge in sex with your friend." He looked at me and laughed and said, "Now I think we should stop our conversation here. Boss will fuck us if we don't reach on time." We both walked towards the meeting room. Jiah joined us on the way, with files in her hand. She always used to wear a sari. She had gotten divorced last year for some reason that no one in the office knew. I did. I still remember our first accidental sex. That took place in the office.

"It might take time, but you both have to finish this work by today only," Boss gave strict instructions to both of us. His voice was so loud that everyone outside knew that we were being smacked. We tried to get help of everyone present, but the others were already overloaded with work and no one was ready to put in extra hours.

"I think we should start at least?" Jiah said.

"I think you should lead, Jiah. I know I am your senior, but you are very well stitched to this project, so I think you should lead," I said.

"You know what Maan, I think you would do good in future. Giving lead to your juniors is such a big deal," she said.

"Jiah, I trust you. I have seen your work, I know what you can do. And there's a lot that I can learn from you," I said.

"Thanks a lot." She smiled at me and took the file in her hands. She was very accurate in her work. We both were deeply involved in our work and time was running by. One by one, people were leaving the office. Only Jiah and I were left in the end.

"Don't you feel scared?" I asked her at around midnight.

"Scared of whom? You?" she asked me, almost amused.

"No, I mean I am scared of the dark. And my water bottle is empty too," I said.

She laughed and said, "You can have water from my bottle." She offered me her bottle and both of us went back to work.

"And finally done…" she said after finishing the last line of the presentation.

"We could finish it just because of you, Jiah. I would not have done it so accurately and sharply without your help," I told her.

"Don't be so good, buddy. It wasn't possible without you. I would say you deserve your position," Jiah said and switched off her computer.

"Jiah, now even your water bottle is empty and the kitchen is a bit far," I said in a requesting tone.

She stood and said, "You are unbelievable!" Then, she went straight to the kitchen.

I heard something falling. It was 2 a.m. and I was scared. I started shivering. My body started getting cold, so I stood up from the chair and ran towards the kitchen.

"Jiah, what happened?" I whispered.

"Why are you whispering?" she said picking up the glass that had fallen down.

"Nothing, I just thought I'd talk to you in a different manner. Wasn't it cool?" I said normally, happy that she was there.

"I know you are scared of the dark, but I'm here. So just chill. Nobody's going to harm you," she told me.

"Thank you! Tell me one thing, are you not afraid of anything?" I asked her.

"Not at all. I've been staying alone for a long time, Maan. I got married to my love five years back. Those were the days when I used to get scared the same way as you are now. Our families were not ready for our marriage. We ran away and got married in a temple. We were too happy together. We proved our decision was right, but god wanted something else.

"With time, we realised that we were not made for each other after all. We used to fight a lot. The reasons behind our fights were quite funny but I think we will talk about that some other day. Above all this, he had his family to share things with. But I was all alone after my family cut all ties with me. I was dead to my parents. But somehow I handled the situation and decided to divorce him. After that I have gone through many sleepless nights because I was scared of being alone. Now I'm used to that," she said.

"So, I'm not the only one who is suffering from such kind of pain," I said.

"I think your wife is still alive." She looked at me with surprise.

"Yeah, yeah. Very much. Can we discuss something else, please?" I tried to change the topic.

She managed to stick to the topic and said, "Actually, I don't want to poke if it makes you uncomfortable. But you can share anything you want with me."

"I think some other day would be better," I said.

"Cool," she replied and offered me a glass of water. I had some water and saw a lizard over the wall, just behind Jiah. I finished my water and thought of scaring Jiah with the lizard.

"Jiah, look over there! Such a beautiful painting na." I made something up to scare her. And I succeeded too. She turned around and shouted like hell and took a few steps back in a hurry. She lost her balance and fell down. I was laughing.

"I'm sorry ma'am, I thought you are not scared of anything." I continued laughing.

"I didn't expect this from you at all, and I'm still fighting to get rid of these ugly lizards." I offered her my hand to get up, but she rejected it and got up by herself. She was barely able to stand properly.

"I think you are hurt."

"I don't think I can even walk now," she said, stumbling to gain balance.

"Just come up to that sofa. I'll get some first aid for you."

"I need your support. I don't think I can take even a single step on my own." She was screaming in pain by now.

"Okay, just take my support and I'll lead you to the sofa." I held her by her waist and she took support of my shoulders.

She managed to reach the sofa with my support. While she was sitting down, I couldn't balance the weight and we both fell on the sofa. Our faces were too close to each other's. Our eyes were talking. Suddenly she kissed me deep. I closed my eyes for a second and let myself go. Something suddenly stopped me and I pushed her back. I got up, having the worst feeling in my heart. I went back a few steps, my back to her. I could feel the blood running through my veins. My whole body wanted this, it seemed. In that one moment, I forgot everything. I ran back to the sofa, held her close and kissed her back. That's where it all began with Jiah.

"I think we should forget this, let's just consider it as an accident," I said while dressing up near the sofa. I knew I had done something wrong. I had changed the earlier job because of this reason. It wasn't possible for me to leave this job too, so soon. Moreover, I was under a contract of one year with this company.

"You are right. Actually I'm sorry to have started," Jiah said.

"No, it's not at all your fault. I think it was just an accident, we should forget it," I said.

"Thank you for understanding me, Maan," she said. We both put our clothes on and went downstairs. We started searching for our vehicles. I pressed the unlock button of my car and located it.

"Oye, Maan! Don't leave me alone here," Sameer shouted from behind me.

"What are you doing here?" I asked, surprised.

"You're not the only one who works in this office, I guess," he said.

"Duffer, he means it's 2 a.m., and our office timings get over at 7 p.m." Jiah said.

"I know Jiah, but how can I leave my friend alone here?" Sameer said. Jiah didn't reply anything and went away to get her bike.

"Where are you going?" Sameer asked her.

"My bike is there."

"It's 2 a.m. Jiah and I don't think we will allow you to go alone on that vehicle. And I think your home is on the way, so we will drop you," Sameer said.

"No thanks, I'm all good."

"Maan, you tell her. In fact, you can pick her up in the morning too," Sameer was trying to convince me, but I was in no mood to say anything to her.

"Jiah, I think he is right. It's better you come with us. I'll pick you up in the morning," I finally said. She didn't reply and just took the front seat. Sameer took the back seat. I drove towards her place. Ninety percent of our conversation was one-sided, that too from Sameer. Jiah and I just used to say yes or no, or just a humming sound of acceptance or rejection to his words. We reached Jiah's place and dropped her.

"What's going on?" Sameer asked me after we dropped Jiah.

"What? I think we are going home," I said.

"Don't try to be over smart. I know something's wrong," he said. I know he was not going to stop asking unless he got the right answer.

"Nothing, it just happened," I said.

"What just happened?" I think he clearly figured it out, but he wanted a clarification.

"Yaar, we didn't want to, but the circumstances were such that we couldn't control ourselves," I said.

"Can you be clear with what you couldn't control," he said.

"Sex!" I became angry and added, "Happy? You wanted to hear that, right?" I screamed at him.

"Are you out of your mind? Clearly, I'm not going to change my job this time."

"I told you, we couldn't control it."

"Yeah, it's simple to say that you couldn't control. Have you ever thought about Kiara? What will happen when she comes to know about it?"

"Sameer, you are over-reacting. Jiah is a nice girl and we have decided to forget everything that happened and treat the incident as an accident. So you don't have to be worried about the job," I explained.

"I don't understand you, Maan. I mean, on the one hand you say that you have the world's best wife. So I can't understand the things you are doing. Anyway it's your life. I don't have the right to judge you or your life choices."

"What do you think, Sameer? That I like all this? No! You know the reason of my leaving earlier jobs. I'm trying my best to come out of this. Of course Kiara is the best wife in this world. But I think I'm looking for Naaz in all those girls. I know that I will never find her. But this stupid mind is not in control."

"Why do you love Naaz so much, yaar? Anyway, my place is here. Drive safely and I'll pray that you come out of this soon," he said and I stopped the car near his house.

Sameer walked out of the car and came close to my side of the window to say, "Even you should pray to god, Maan. He always gives you what you want."

"You are right, Sameer. Even I have experienced that," I slowly came out of the car.

"Really? I didn't know that," he said surprised.

"It's just that every time I got intimate with Naaz was just because I prayed to god for it. But every time I prayed, there was a small sentence added to my wish…"

"And what was that?"

"At least once, please. Send her to me only once. And to my surprise, he always listened to me. In fact, it was after these incidents only that I started believing in god so strongly. And lastly, when I prayed that I wanted her for a lifetime, god didn't listen to me."

"And because of that you think now god doesn't listen to you?"

"No, it's not that. I believe in god. When Naaz was not giving any signs of loving me, I asked god to remove Naaz from my life. And it seems like he did it." Tears started flowing down without permission.

"Life is not over yet, Maan. You can ask to get Naaz back in your life and everything will be okay."

"How can you say that, Sameer? Everything's messed up now. It feels like cheating Kiara. I can't leave her like that. You know what Sameer, I have promised her that I won't leave her alone in life. I have chosen my life and now my life means Kiara's life too. I can't ask for anything from god now."

"There would be some way out, Maan," Sameer said.

"Actually there is something. Wait…" I closed both my eyes and joined my hands and prayed out loud. "God, please call me to you. I think that's the only solution for me in this life. Everyone will be happy." My voice broke at the end.

Sameer hugged me and said, "No, no, Maan! You should not say that. We still need you in this world. Just take back your words, Maan. Life will lead you to some beautiful turns."

We heard a sudden thunder and it started pouring. Sameer took me to the driver's seat and told me to calm down and reach home safely. Sameer was really a true friend to me. I don't know why but I used to share everything with him. Everyone should have at least one friend like Sameer or Mehul in their life. I was lucky to have such amazing friends.

❖

I drove back home with a tired face. My wife opened the door with a big smile on her face. "You look so tired. Let me get something to drink for you."

"No, Kiara. I'm fine and thanks for asking, I would rather go to bed. Even tomorrow morning I have to leave early."

"Don't you think your boss is giving you a lot of work? Working so late and going so early…" said concerned.

"No Kiara, sometimes we have to work more and this is the only time when you prove yourself. Boss hasn't called us early, I have to pick Jiah on the way."

"Jiah? Who is she?"

"Jealous?" I said amused. "Don't worry, she is just a colleague. We both were working on a project together."

"Why would I be jealous? By the way, you two were alone in the office?" Her doubts were increasing.

"No, Sameer was there," I lied a bit.

"Okay, he is the same guy who is changing jobs with you? Such a true friend," she sounded relieved.

"Yeah, now can we just go to bed. I need to sleep."

We both went to bed. My mind was still stuck on her question. I had never lied to Kiara, and this was the first time. My guilt was very strong. I thought of telling her the truth, but also knew that it might ruin the situation.

"Wake up, Maan! You are getting late. Jiah must be waiting." Kiara woke me up in the morning lovingly.

"You are quite worried about Jiah. Aren't you scared of her?" I said sleepily.

"You are still talking about last night! I shouldn't have said that. I'm sorry honey," she said with a sorry face.

"I'm a little upset, but I have an option now. I can go to Jiah; she might understand me," I tried to tease her.

"If you are going to try anything like that, I'll kill you. And I swear I'll do that." She came over the bed saying this. Before I could say anything, she shut my mouth with a kiss.

"Get ready, I'll make some breakfast for you," she said turning back to the kitchen. I looked at her and thought how very innocent she was! The things I was doing to her were so wrong.

"You are always in a hurry. Try to wake up fifteen minutes earlier so that you can finish your breakfast." She shouted from behind me as I rushed for work.

I reached Jiah's apartment and pressed the doorbell. I waited for some time but there was no response. I did that again and was met with silence again. I tried it the third time and she opened the door, hiding behind the door.

"Come inside!" I think she was not dressed properly.

"No, I'll wait outside. You can finish up and come out."

"Don't create a scene in the lobby; just come inside!" She said in anger. I saw that she was only in her blouse and petticoat.

"You have a seat. I'll get ready in five minutes." She went inside the room and locked the door from inside. Just after a few minutes, she came out in a pink sari, her wet hair.

"Tea or coffee?"

"Nothing, I had my breakfast."

"Come on! I can't have it all alone. You have to give me company." She insisted.

"Okay, then I think coffee will work better." She went to the kitchen and made coffee for both of us.

"Can I ask you a question?" I said.

"Go ahead."

"Why did you get divorced? You can tell me if you are comfortable. I mean, if you have any problem in sharing, don't."

"No, I don't have any problem. But promise me you won't laugh."

"Okay, I promise I won't laugh."

"Most of the time, he wanted his mom to sleep with us." Before I could start laughing, she started off in loud guffaws. Looking at her, I couldn't stop laughing.

"Sorry but you broke my promise," I said. "And what about his mom? She was okay with it?"

"I mean, she used to be fine."

"OMG! I don't believe this. You can't be serious! And how did you allow that?"

"Actually it was okay for once. But her mom could not leave him alone. So she kept on asking to sleep with us. And later on, I was not ready for that at all. Things started getting worse. I tried hard to control the situation, but nothing worked. I messed up everything." She started sounding low and I thought she would cry.

"Hey, hey, hey! Please don't start crying now." I kept the cup on the table and took place next to her, trying to calm her down. She hugged me tightly and started crying. I was pulled down unknowingly as she hugged me and this time, she fell over me. We did not want to, but I don't get why these things are always beyond control.

It was a steamy session and we had forgotten everything.

"I think we shouldn't have done this," she told me while hooking up her blouse.

"I know but I think this was the last time. Next time we won't be able to have such alone time or a place. It was all because we were alone," I said.

"We are already late. Boss would be waiting for us."

We work together and she used to live alone in her apartment. Obviously we got much of alone time to spend together and mistakes happened again and again.

❖

Now, after all these months, I wanted to get rid of Jiah. And that too without having to change the job. I was having a good package and a good position too. Jiah was holding her files in her hands, ready for the meeting. I knew Sameer was trying to find someone special. I got an idea to get rid of Jiah. A sudden smile came up on my face.

"Why are you smiling?" Jiah asked.

"Nothing." I looked at her and kept smiling. We all went to the meeting room and I was continuously starring at Jiah and Sameer. They did look good together. Not only that, they both needed a partner too. The biggest problem was convincing them.

"Again overloaded with work, Maan. I don't know when our boss will give us a breather," Jiah said after the meeting.

"You will get relief soon," I said with a smiling face.

"You are still smiling; something is going on in your mind," Jiah said.

"I have seen him smiling like this after years, Jiah. Let him," Sameer said.

"No, but he is behaving weird," Jiah said making a strange face. Jiah went back to her desk, and I went to mine.

"What's wrong Maan? And stop smiling, please!" Sameer said.

"You know what! I have found a girl for you."

"And shall I know who she is?"

"Stand up!" I said.

"Why? Don't tell me that she's from our office."

"Just stand up, yaar." I held him from his shoulder and made him stand up. I pointed my finger towards Jiah and said, "Look at that girl!"

"Who? Jiah?" Sameer's voice rose up a bit. Jiah heard him and looked at us. I again smiled and waved my hand. She smiled with a really confused expression and waved back.

"Are you nuts? Why are you shouting?" I pushed Sameer back into his chair.

"Obviously my reaction would be of that kind," he whispered.

"Why? Don't you like her?"

"Maan, I think you are out of your mind. You have slept with her, and not just once. And now you are bringing her proposal to me. I think you need to give your mind some rest." He turned back to his computer screen.

"Forget about me and Jiah. You guys should get married. I promise I won't even look at her. You know all those were accidents. She is alone, and needs company."

"I can understand her part, but what about you? You have your wife. Your sexual life with your wife is good too. Then why Jiah?"

"To understand this, you have to fall in love once. I think I'm trying to find Naaz everywhere. May be in every girl. And I know that I won't find a match in any of these girls. But some things are always beyond control. I didn't want to be with Jiah; something was attracting me towards her."

"So, to get rid of her, you are pairing me with her? What a great idea!" Sameer said.

"Yeah, I admit that I want to stay away from her, but I know that you won't have a better option than her. Just look at her and give yourself a chance. You are my best friend and I won't think bad for you." I made Sameer look at Jiah once again. He stared at her for a few seconds.

"But…"

"Leave these ifs and buts. Just tell me, is she good or not?"

"She is, but what about her? Is she interested in me?" Sameer was getting convinced slowly.

"You leave that to me. Just tell me if you are okay with her?"

"You know what, I haven't seen such a *kamina* friend in my life. You are offering me a girl with whom you have slept. Keep in mind that I'm only saying yes to get you out of her." I was glad Sameer was convinced. For that matter, I knew Jiah was a nice girl. Whatever was happening between us was not at all comfortable.

"Hey, what happened?" Sameer asked me.

"Nothing man, I am just happy that you said yes."

"I want to ask you a question."

I just nodded my head in a yes and he asked me, "Do you have any feelings for Jiah? I mean, I know you, but you might have found a replacement for Naaz."

"Sameer, you don't have to be worried about anything. God has given me plenty of options in life. But till now, Kiara has been the best. Even after finding the best replacement for Naaz in my mind, god kept giving me more options. And I know, that journey is not going to stop until I get Naaz back into my life. Looking at the present situation, I don't think Naaz will come back. But still, somewhere my heart says that she will come."

"I think the same happened with Naaz too. You became physical with her and then you realized that you love her. I'm afraid that this can again happen with Jiah. I'm asking this because you haven't thought of changing the job this time."

"Oh god, as for changing the job, tell me Sameer… Which company will give us such a good salary? And you don't remember I guess, but we have signed a contract with the company. You know very well that we can't leave the company like that."

"Contract? I think you have forgotten that we had contracts with our earlier companies too. I can believe you on the salary bit. You are right. I think no other company will give us a better salary for our current credentials," he answered. "But again, I want to ask you, are you sure you won't fall in love with Jiah?"

"Do you know the definition of love? According to me, love cannot be defined. You can feel love. You can live love. I know and understand love only because of Naaz. No other human can take her place in my life," I said.

"I should not say this, but I think if this ever happened to me, I won't be able to live. I might commit suicide. How can you live without a person you love so much?"

"You know why I am still living? Because I'm happy that Naaz accepted my love for that one night in Aman's friend's flat. That one moment of my life is the reason for me to live. I still want my life to drive me back to that moment and pause there for a lifetime. And being specific, I'm not that big a coward to commit suicide. I won't ever take my life, but I have asked for death from god for sure. Let's see when he accepts my request," I wiped off my bloody tears.

"We still need you, duffer! And god knows that, so he won't take you back so easily. I don't know when I'll get that kind of love in my life."

"Don't you ever wish for a life like me, Sameer. You might be feeling that having true love in life is amazing, but it is very difficult. I'm alive because of that one moment. I tried to avoid speaking with her every day, many times, but I couldn't stop. Those chats are keeping me alive. That hope of her coming back into my life is keeping me alive. This period is very painful for my heart."

"I'm amazed that you guys still talk every day and are not ready to admit your love. Don't you think you should make it clear with her… whether it is a yes or a no? Once and for all," Sameer said.

"I have tried many times, you know. She stops talking to me for a few days after that. I can't afford that. I don't want to lose her friendship."

"Maan, everything will be fine, brother."

"Honestly, Sameer, I know that there is very little hope of her coming back now. Leave all this bullshit and let's come back to Jiah. I think you two would make a good pair."

"But buddy, I'm a bit nervous. What if she says no?"

"You know if I'll ask her, she'll definitely say no, and might not even talk to you for the rest of your life," I said.

"I think you are right. Then what should we do?"

"*We*? I think you have to do this on your own."

"No, but you said that you'll take care of her part."

"Umm, looks like I have changed my mind."

"You can't do this to me. You have to help me."

"We can do one thing – I'll help you backstage, but you'll be the leader."

Sameer agreed on that. "So, what we are supposed to do now?" Sameer asked.

"Right now, I think you should focus on your work and let me think what we can do."

"You know, I haven't seen you so happy and so helpful ever in the past. Thank you very much," Sameer said sincerely.

"You want me to help you, right?" He just nodded his head and I added, "Then just do your work and let me think. Don't use these stupid words like thank you and all," I said. He mock saluted me like a jawan would to his leader and got back to work.

"So, any ideas?" Sameer asked me during lunch time while we walked towards the office canteen.

"Just shut up! I have work to do, so I couldn't get time for thinking about this."

"You don't have time to think over it? What a waste of a friend you are!"

"Buddy, you might be the most intelligent programmer in this office but when it comes to girls, no one is as good as me. And let me make it very clear, girls don't like workaholic people. They do love intelligence, but you have to show them. I have to think of something really good for you. Tell me, why are you being so desperate? In the morning you were not even ready to consider her, and look at you now!" I whispered with anger.

"Okay, can we order something?" Sameer diverted my attention.

I nodded and looked around for an empty table. In just another second, I found Jiah sitting all alone at a table, having her coffee.

"Sameer, get your coffee and take a seat next to Jiah over there. I'll manage my coffee on my own," I said, pointing a finger towards Jiah. "And try to speak with her."

"Okay, but what will I talk about?" Sameer looked confused and nervous.

"Anything! You can start your conversation with a comment like 'Nice coffee' or something. But for that you have to go there. So don't waste your time or she'll finish her coffee."

Sameer ran to get a cup of coffee. He ordered one and reached the table where Jiah was seated. I could see that his hands were shivering. He sat in front of Jiah and cleared his throat to get attention.

"Nice coffee," he said.

"I don't think you have tasted it yet," Jiah said.

I didn't know what Sameer was going to do now. Now I understood that even experts like Sameer can make mistakes when they change their field. I just wanted to go there and slap him hard.

"No, actually I always have coffee here. So I know it's good," with those words, he started shivering more and took a sip of his coffee. "I think I should go now," he was really nervous.

"No, I think you should finish your coffee," she said kindly.

"No, but it's bit ho.. ho.. hot." I could see that he was becoming more nervous with every breath he took in front of Jiah.

"Yeah, I could see that. You can wait till it cools down a little." Sameer just nodded his head and waited for a few seconds. But the nervousness was increasing, and he started sweating profusely.

"Do you need some water?" Jiah asked.

"Yes." Sameer picked up the water bottle which was already there on the table and added some water to his coffee. And without wasting a minute, he picked up the coffee mug which was overflowing and drank it in one gulp.

"Okay bye." He did not even wait for her response. The worst first meeting ever. Now I understood why Sameer was still unmarried.

"Are you out of your mind?" I asked him when he came to me. "You had such a good opportunity, no one was around. And why the hell were you shivering?"

"Look, Maan, I won't be able to do this. I have never spoken to a woman like that." He went out without saying much. Now what? I think I should give it time. Only because Jiah needed to forget this meeting.

In the days that followed, I tried to get Jiah and Sameer together many times, but Sameer was not ready to talk to her. Even Jiah was occupied at work.

"Maan I don't know what it is, but I am having some problem in running this program. It's not giving me proper output." She shared her query one day. We both tried for a few minutes, but still something was missing. I was thinking about the problem when my eyes landed on Sameer.

"Sameer! I think he can solve this," I said out loud.

"Who? Your friend?"

"Yeah, I think he can do this."

"Who, that dumbo? I met him a few days back in the canteen. I don't know for what reason he was shivering so much. And can you imagine he drinks coffee by mixing water in it?" She started laughing.

"You think he is dumb? Let me make it clear that he is one of the most intelligent people in the whole office. I can bet you on that," I said confidently.

"I don't believe that," Jiah said just as surely.

"You will believe me when he makes this program work properly."

"Maan, I bet you he won't be able to do that."

"Okay, then let's make a deal. If he does this, you will go on a date with him."

"Done, and if he doesn't, you will go on a date with Shila."

"Okay done! I know she won't come with me at all. You should have thought before you said this, Jiah."

"Don't worry, Maan. She told me yesterday that she has a crush on you."

Now this had become a serious thing. I was praying that Sameer could finish the program. I called him to the table and explained the problem we were facing. He just smiled at me and said, "Easy". He started punching some keys on the computer.

Jiah and I were looking at the computer screen, but suddenly he stood up and said, "This won't fix, sorry!"

"Sameer, you are a genius. You can't give up so easily," I said. He didn't listen to me and headed back to his seat.

"So, what time will be suitable for Shila?" Jiah started making faces at me. Before I could answer it, Sameer came back.

"Wait a minute!" He again started working and my hopes of winning came back too. "And that's it! Your program is ready guys. Without any error," Sameer said beaming with happiness.

"Let me check," Jiah said and got to work.

"Well, well, well... you did it. I underestimated you. I would like to invite you for dinner, Sameer."

Before Sameer could reply to Jiah, I jumped in between and said, "Why not! He'll be happy."

Sameer was an intelligent guy and I had presumed that Jiah won't be impressed by his knowledge. But the scene was different now. Jiah was getting impressed. I was scared that Sameer would start shivering even on the date. But just because of one program, his energy had been boosted. He was on top of the world. He didn't make his first date the last one, but they went for a few more. Now, it was my turn to do something for them.

# 8

# The Good News

"There's good news, Maan." Kiara told me while serving hot paranthas one morning.

"I know Sameer is getting married. He must have called you," I said.

"What? Sameer is getting married? He didn't tell me. Let him come home and I will take his case. By the way, since when do *you* know that?" The gun point was on me now.

"I just came to know yesterday," I lied.

"Look what kind of friends you have. They don't even share things with you."

"Hold on! What good news were you talking about?" I asked her.

She started smiling at that. I mean, it was a shy smile that I couldn't make head or tail of.

"Why are you smiling Kiara?"

"Actually, I'm not sure, but I think I'm pregnant," she said. That brought that irritating smile on my face too.

"Have you been to a doctor?"

"No, but I used the kit at home and it showed a positive result".

"Okay, then we should go to a doctor and confirm the result." I held her in my arms and said, "Thank you so much for giving me this amazing news." Without wasting any time, we went to the doctor. My mom was desperate to know where we were going. But we decided to not tell anyone unless we were sure.

The doctor took Kiara behind the curtains. I was not allowed to even stand there. After a few seconds, Kiara shouted like someone had pinched her hard.

"Is everything okay, Kiara?" I asked from outside.

"Yes, everything's fine." The doctor came out and said, "Congratulations, you are going to be parents."

Kiara came out from behind the curtain and we looked at each other. I could see happiness on her face. She held my hands and we took a seat opposite the doctor. He gave us some basic information to take care about. And then we drove back to home.

"You go and give the news to Mom," I said to Kiara after we got back from the clinic.

"Are you mad? How I can give the news to her?"

"Then? You expect me to tell my mom? No way."

"Come out of the car, Maan," she said strictly.

"No, I'm getting late for office. Bye! Love you and best of luck." I drove off, leaving her at the gate. I was not able to stop smiling at all. It felt like an achievement to me. I wanted to share this news with someone. I picked up the phone and went to the contacts list. I touched the screen where Naaz was written.

Wait, wait! I shouldn't call Naaz. Kiara is pregnant and I have to forget Naaz I dropped the call and focused on driving. It had been so long and the fact that I had been unable to get Naaz out of my mind was disturbing. But, she was my friend. I shared every good and bad news with her. And there was nothing wrong in sharing this kind of news anyway.

Naaz had become a part of my life. She knew everything about me – my friends, my family and what not. She hadn't even met some of my friends, but knew them so well from our conversations that even if she met them accidently, she would recognise each one of them.

But now the time had come to maintain some distance with her. Now I was going to be a father and my life was going to change. I don't know how that baby would look or whether it would be a boy or a girl. What would be the name?

❖

"Hey, why are you smiling? You came late and look at you! You don't even feel bad about the delay. Boss was asking for you. I told him that your wife had some health issues and you have taken her to the doctor. Just keep this in mind if he asks, our answers should not differ," Sameer said when I reached office.

"What if I say you have given the right reason," I said.

"What do you mean? Is everything okay with Kiara?" He got a bit worried.

"Yes, everything's okay. Actually, it is too good."

"Will you tell me what's hiding behind that smile?"

"I am going to be a father."

"Oh shit!" he shouted out of happiness, and then realized that his voice was too loud. So he started whispering to me and said, "Congratulations bro! I mean, you have given me the best news yaar."

"I'm so happy, Sameer. I think god has given me some relief. First, you and Jiah are getting married, and I'm going to have a child. Truly man, now I believe everything is going to be good."

"You shared this news with Naaz?"

"No, I thought of staying away from her now onwards."

"Seriously? I can't believe this! If you are going to do this, I bet you will be the happiest person in the world. Please Maan, this is the time Kiara needs your complete support."

"Hey guys what's going on?" Jiah interrupted us.

"This stupid fellow is going to be a father! Can you imagine that?" Sameer said.

"That's great news, Maan. Many congratulations buddy."

"Actually I always wondered why people congratulate you for having unprotected sex with your wife," I said.

"Don't say that," Jiah interrupted with disappointment in her tone. "Just go and meet people who don't conceive even after so many trials. Imagine you and Kiara in that place. What if you two had to go through such a situation?"

"I can't even imagine that. And I'm sorry, I take my words back. Thanks for making me understand the depth of this miracle. And thanks for your wishes, guys. Tonight, we are having dinner together," I said and made a call to Kiara.

"Hello Kiara! You want to meet Jiah, right? Let's go out tonight? You can use as many harsh words for Sameer as you want. I'll be there at seven… hope you will be ready by then?"

"It seems you have shared the news with the entire city already. Don't worry, I'll be ready. See you, bye."

"Guys, my days are changing." I told both my besties.

I couldn't work properly that day. Everything was very beautiful all around me. I wanted to explode with happiness. I thought I should inform Naaz. At least as a friend. No, no! I think I should control my feelings and should get rid of this bloody thought. Naaz is my past and now I have to accept the truth.

"Maan, you go and get Kiara to the restaurant. We will be there in an hour," Sameer said before leaving the office. Naaz was still on my mind. But I had decided to not call her. I took my car out and started driving for home. As a cruel twist of fate, I got a call from Naaz. Seeing her name on the screen, I couldn't stop myself and without wasting a second, I picked it up.

"Hey Maan, you must be busy in office. But today I left early, so just called you," Naaz said.

"No, it's okay Naaz. I'm not in office, I'm driving back home."

"How come so early today?"

"Do I need to tell you everything?" I said.

"Of course! I'm not going to leave you so easily. Even god doesn't want us to stop chatting. That's why god planned an early relief for both of us. Can't you see that? And above all, I'm your best friend who knows everything about you, and *will* know everything about you."

"You are making me puke out everything, Naaz. You know what, you are a typical woman!"

"Hey, I am a woman! What is so typical in that?"

"I mean, most women are really talkative and get all personal things out of you by their words. You literally fit over there. Typical woman!" I tried to tease her.

"Not at all, I'm not like that. Just tell me if you want to, else I'm hanging up." It worked.

"Okay, I'll tell you everything, but just calm down first."

"I'm not angry at all."

"I don't understand why you girls never admit that you are angry."

"Do you want to make me angry now? I told you I'm not angry. And don't change the topic." She got angry again. I knew she was not going to admit it at all. I had to tell her.

I cleared my throat and said, "I'm going to be a father."

Listening to this, she started shouting.

"Anything wrong, ma'am?" I heard some other man's voice in her background. Someone must have got a wrong signal from her.

"Just go and do your own work," she told the man off. "Congratulation, Maan. I need a party." she said to me.

"Party? I think you have forgotten that you are in a different state."

"I'm not asking for a party from you. I just said I need a party. And I'll throw the party. You are not the only friend to me; I do have some other friends with whom I can celebrate."

"Great, if you are throwing a party, even I can join in. Just send me the air fare."

"Ha, ha, ha very funny. Now take very good care of Kiara and congratulate her on my behalf. I have reached home. Bye, will call you later."

"Even I'm about to reach home. Take care, bye."

I don't know why but I felt uncomfortable in talking to Naaz when I was at home. And I think even she felt that way. Actually

I know why I felt uncomfortable; it was because I loved her. But she, why was she behaving like that? She always disconnected the call when she was about to reach home. These very small things made me feel that she too loved me, but was not admitting it. And I couldn't stop talking to her in the hope that someday, she will say something to me.

"Good evening Mom. Where's Kiara? Is she ready?" My mom opened the door when I reached home.

"What's so good about this evening? Your wife doesn't listen to me. I'm shouting since morning, but who's going to listen to this old lady." The matter looked serious.

"Mom, what happened?"

"Ask your wife." She shouted at me.

"Kiara..." I called out to her and she came down on my second call.

"What's wrong Kiara? You two have never fought. Is there anything wrong?"

"Your mom is not leaving me since morning. You asked me to share the good news with her, and I did. But look what she is doing! Ever since she has known that I'm pregnant, her reaction has suddenly changed. She is throwing fire crackers at me since morning."

"Behave Kiara! She's my Mom," I said to Kiara and turned back to mom. "Mom, what's this? You know she's pregnant!"

"I know she's pregnant, that's why I don't want her to work. I told her to take rest. But she's not listening to me at all. She kept on doing house work," Mom said.

"Maan, you tell me, how can I let her work at this age?" Kiara said before I could answer Mom.

"You always think I'm old. So old that I can't even take care of you." Mom threw another bomb from her arsenal. Both of them were not allowing me to talk.

"Stop guys, please stop! Are you guys out of your mind? You found this topic to fight? Seriously?"

"But she is…" Kiara tried to interrupt me, but I stopped her.

"Listen to me first. I have a way out for this. Let us hire a maid. So, both of you will get rest. And both of you need that. And Kiara, get ready! They must be waiting." Suddenly both of them started laughing.

"Maan, we already came to this solution," Kiara said .

"Then what was all the drama?"

"My dear son, if we had asked you directly for a maid, you would have rejected the proposal. So, we created this scene. I was the script writer, and Kiara added suggestions," Mom said it like she has done some great work.

"Great, Mom! But you haven't understood me, it seems. This drama was not needed. By the way, where did you find a maid so quickly?"

"Wait!" Mom shouted out looking at the kitchen, "Shila!"

To my surprise, our office maid was at our home now.

"What are you doing here? How did you guys find her?" I was taken aback at the coincidence.

"Actually I asked Sameer for suggesting someone and he asked Shila to find someone for us. But instead of sending someone, she came over herself," Kiara said.

"And what about office? Boss will kill me," I said.

"Don't worry. Shila arranged for another maid for your office," Mom said. Now I knew that Jiah was right about Shila.

She really had a crush on me, it seems. But looking at the current situation, I had to give approval.

"Okay fine, whatever works for all you women. Kiara, please get ready and come. I'm waiting in the car."

"Thank you. You are very sweet," Kiara said.

I hate this word sweet, and especially when it is used for a human. I don't know why, but I do.

We reached the restaurant in the next twenty minutes or so. Sameer and Jiah were already there.

"You are so useless, Sameer," Kiara straightaway pounced on Sameer with her words. "You didn't tell me about Jiah. Since when is all this going on between you guys?"

"Maan knows everything, from the very beginning. Hasn't he talked about us? Actually he is the one who helped us get closer." Kiara turned to me with a strange expression, but I stared at my feet to avoid her gaze.

"By the way, this is Jiah. And Jiah, she is Kiara, Maan's wife." Sameer said.

"Maan knew that?" She turned to me. "Maan what is this, how could you lie to me? You said that you came to know yesterday." Her anger was growing.

"No, it's not that Kiara. I didn't lie to you. I actually helped them to be together, but I came to know about his marriage yesterday only. Right, Sameer?" I tried to explain.

Sameer said, "Yes, Kiara, he didn't know about the marriage."

"You guys do play very well. This time I'm letting you go, but next time, I'll kill you both," Kiara warned us and turned to Jiah. "Jiah, you are so beautiful. But please learn to handle these guys. They are insane. You must be aware of this already, I am sure because you work with them."

"Ya, Kiara they are super bad boys." Her words supported Kiara's sentences totally. Now the G-talk was not going to end. Even at our dinner table, Sameer and I could hardly speak.

"You girls enjoy your chit-chat, we will go for a walk," I said after dinner.

"Thank you, Maan, I was getting bored. We were four, but I was feeling all alone over there." Sameer said after we left the table.

"Even I was getting bored. So, tell me, how life's going with Jiah?"

"It's all a dream for me. Thanks to you. If you hadn't helped me speak up to Jiah, I would have become like you, dying every day to get love."

"You are the lucky one, dude!"

"Don't worry, man. Even your life will be good now. I can feel the vibe," Sameer said.

"Hoping is good. I don't have any other option anyway. By the way, Sameer, I want to say something to you. No, just leave it."

"What? Go ahead, man."

"Nothing, just leave it!"

"Did you sleep with Jiah again or what?" Sameer asked suddenly.

"No loser, don't even think about that now! We are not interested in each other. And I just wanted to tell you that I talked to Naaz today."

"Oh god, why am I with this guy? You told me you won't call her. I was so happy with your decision, and now you ruined everything."

"I know, but I didn't call. She was the one who called me up. Otherwise I was sure of not calling her."

"Seriously, you could have ignored the call. I know even you were desperate to talk to her since morning."

"I think you are right, man. I couldn't control. You know how much I love Naaz."

"I am very disappointed with you, Maan. You might be in love with anyone in this world but I can say one thing clearly – you are cheating on Kiara. Look at her Maan, she's madly in love with you. You are doing same with Kiara what Naaz is doing with you. Being with you, but not having you. I think you should give your life a thought."

"These things are very easy to say, but be in my shoes for a bit and then say. Think about you not getting married to Jiah and to someone else. Can't even think, right? Would you be able to love again?"

"Truly speaking, if I had to choose between Naaz and Kiara, I would choose Kiara. You don't even know if Naaz loves you or not. Please don't do this to Kiara; she won't be able to handle this. Now just give yourself some time and think." Then after a moment, he said, "The girls must be waiting. I think we should go back. And Maan, Kiara is pregnant. Please take care of her. Don't ever let her know about you and Naaz."

"Okay. I would stop talking to Naaz, but do you think I'll be able to love Kiara in the same way? Never Sameer, never. I won't be able to love Kiara at all."

"I agree that you won't be able to love her. But at least allow her to love you. Don't break her heart. She is a good person. That is all I have to say."

"Seems you guys had a great time," Jiah said as we reached the table.

"Yeah, it's been long that we had such a leisure time. Thank you guys, for such amazing food and company! I think we should do this often," Sameer said.

"What? Making Kiara pregnant?" I joked.

"I don't mind that." Sameer said.

We all laughed out loud at that. I know Sameer was right that night. But I couldn't figure out where I was wrong. My life was becoming full on dramatic with each passing day. I left it all on god. I don't know what other surprises he had planned for me.

# 9

# Reality

"Thank you very much for coming a day earlier. I thought you won't come," I said to Sameer when we got some free time on the terrace.

"Why not! It's Kiara's baby shower. You asked for help; how could I say no?" Sameer said.

"I thought you still have something in your mind about me and Jiah, so you might not come," I spoke in a low voice.

"Stop embarrassing me, yaar. It was my fault and you know that. I'm sorry. I should not have questioned my best friend."

"Can I ask you one thing? What made you think so? I mean why did you think that Jiah and I were still together?" I dared to ask him.

"Just because I love Jiah. I was feeling insecure. Maan, I come from a family where girls don't have much freedom. They generally don't talk much with guys, or even if they do, it is limited. If the guy has taken a decision, she has to follow the decision blindly. Jiah is totally opposite to that. She is bold, she take her own decisions.

I started feeling low. I felt like I don't even exist in my house. Days after marriage were tough on me too. I somehow managed to show her I was happy at home, but outside, she was too friendly with other men. She started creating better relationships with my friends. Maan, she was spending so much time with you. I knew that boss had given work to both of you. But still I got jealous of you. Your past with Jiah started irking my mind. I tried hard to take that thought out of my mind, but I couldn't. And now, I'm happy that everything is clear and I got everything back."

"How did you realize that we are innocent and it was your wrong mindset?"

"From day one, I knew it was my fault. I knew that Jiah and you don't have any relationship now. But I think I was feeling insecure. As I told you, I was scared of losing her. Do you remember when I fought with you in front of so many people? I still remember that. Maan, that was the biggest mistake of my life. I lost my best friend on that day. You stopped talking to me from that day. Actually, I became happy that day onwards because Jiah started keeping distance from you to save our relationship.

"Another mistake I made was that I started doing this to everyone who was in touch with her. And she was so good that she didn't fight for her rights, for her freedom. One day, she left the house leaving a letter for me. You know what she had written? She wrote 'Sorry, I could not make you happy'. The truth was that I couldn't make her happy. To satisfy my ego, I didn't even talk to her for at least fifteen days. I realized her value after losing her. I had so many sleepless nights. Life became hell for me. I'm sorry, Maan, I'm really sorry." He couldn't stop himself from crying.

"Thank god you realized what love is! You only understand love well when you are away from your loved one. You came to know about her value in your life." Even I was feeling sad at hearing him.

Sameer hugged me and said, "Thank you for being my friend again. I am happy that everything is sorted out. Let's just finish some pending works buddy; tomorrow morning is your day."

"Look at me! Before you got married, I had promised you that there won't be anything between me and Jiah; we will be just friends. To be specific, I never break promises." I said and both of us went for finishing some decoration part.

Kiara and Jiah were staying in one room, and Sameer and I in another.

"You don't snore, right?" I asked Sameer before going to bed.

"I don't know. You'll come to know tonight."

"Seriously Sameer, if you snore, I'll throw you out of the room."

"Haha, I was just joking. But the same thing applies to you too." Sameer told me, and then asked me, "Shall I ask you one thing?"

"Hmm."

"You still loves Naaz, right?"

"Sameer, this is not the time to discuss this. I'm sleepy, we can talk about it tomorrow." I tried to avoid answering.

"That means you still love her. I understand now how much difficult it would be for you. You must have invited her for the function?"

"Sameer, can you please stop putting your logic to everything! Naaz is not invited."

"What the hell! Why didn't you invite her?"

"Sameer, I have to keep a budget in mind. So, I haven't called any of my friends."

"You have invited me," Sameer said.

"You are more like a brother to me and not just a friend. And seriously, I was not expecting you'd come."

"Ha ha very funny. I think you are lying. You haven't called her because you love her and you can't hide your feelings from her."

"You are sick, please let me sleep. I have a lot to do in the morning." I was trying to avoid his questions, but he kept continuing with the same. I stopped replying and acted like I was in a deep sleep. But even then, he didn't stop. After a few minutes, he finally slept off.

"What happened buddy? What was that sound? Is that a terrorist attack or what?" Sameer and I woke up together to the sound of a blast. We looked around and I saw that somebody have fired a cracker in my room. I saw some portion of a joss stick too.

"This means they are here!" I told myself.

"Who?" Sameer thought I was talking to him. I didn't reply but went to the bathroom and filled a bucket with water.

"Now they have to pay for this," I said.

"Maan, I'm scared. Can you please tell me what's going on? And why the hell you are filling that bucket?"

"Sameer, take one bucket. I'll tell you everything after we are done." We both went out with our buckets full.

"They must have come at night. And there was only one room left in this house, where they would be," I said.

"Maan, what are you talking about, yaar?"

"Nothing! You just follow me." We reached near the room.

"There's no one in this room, Maan," Sameer said.

"Let me check." I opened the door slowly so that it didn't make any sound. I could see some people sleeping on the bed. "I told you they will be here."

"I'm really scared now. Who are these people?"

"Don't be scared. I'll take all the responsibility of whatever happens. Just follow me and we have to empty this bucket on them."

"Why?" Sameer asked again.

"Stop asking questions!" Both of us went there and we threw all the water on the people sleeping over there. And to our surprise, it was some relatives of mine who had come a day earlier to attend the function. One of the uncles stood up from the bed and said, "I didn't expect this from you. Even children don't do this kind of fun. Tell me on my face if you don't want me here or any of us to attend the function." He was really angry.

"Sorry uncle, I didn't want to do that to you. I thought my friends were sleeping in this room. And uncle, I had given you a different room. How could I even imagine that you would be here?" I knew my friends would have sent them here.

"You wanted to throw this water on your friends? Shame on you Maan! They are so good. They convinced us to take this room because it is more airy. See Maan, I don't want to argue with you. And I don't want to spoil the function, but whatever you have done is very wrong."

All of them stood up from there and went out. And my devil friends entered the room with a heavy laughter.

"Stop laughing guys. This was horrible!" I said.

"Hey Maan, congratulations yaar. You didn't attend our baby shower, but we are attending yours. And that too without your invitation," Nayra said.

"Guys, it's a working day and I thought you won't be able to manage." I tried to explain.

"You duffer! I think your wife is better than you. She told us to give you a surprise. And this was your punishment for not inviting us." Naaz came out from behind Aman. Now how could I say that I didn't call anybody just because of her? So, now the baby shower was going to have some twists and turns.

"You are Naaz, right? Very pretty," Sameer said.

"Maan, I think you should introduce us," Naaz turned to me.

"Sorry guys, this was all so messy that I forgot to introduce you. Sameer, these are my friends from college – Mehul, Nayra, Aman and Naaz." I introduced my friends to Sameer and then continued, "Guys, this is Sameer, my colleague-cum-friend. We have worked together for more than three years."

"You are very handsome, I tell you," Naaz said to Sameer and winked at me.

"Thank you, but I'm married." All of us laughed and we decided to not sleep that night and just talk. We were talking about each other's life. It has been too long and we didn't know much about each other's lives.

"So Naaz, what's going on in your life?" I asked her.

"Nothing much. I think you know about me. We usually talk."

"Yes, but you might have hidden something like I did. I didn't tell you about my wife's baby shower."

"I'm not married or I would have kept my husband's baby shower a secret." Naaz was in the mood to spread happiness, but behind her jokes, I could see that she was hiding something.

"Very funny, but I was asking about your marriage, or your boyfriend, or you are not getting married at all?"

"You know, I think that's a great idea… not getting married. If Sameer was not married, I would have thought about him."

"Thanks Naaz, but according to me, if you have ever felt anything for anybody in this world, you should go to that person and confess your feelings. Otherwise it would be very late, Sameer said.

"Sometimes it's better to keep silent," Naaz said and looked at me. That gave me a sign that she might be talking about our relationship, but it was better to not talk about it. Maybe she was right, sometimes it's better to stay silent.

"I agree with you Naaz. I made a mistake by accepting Aman's proposal. I should have been silent at that time," Nayra said and everyone shared a little laughter.

"Oh my god, I'm sorry guys, but I have forgotten to test the lights. It's 5 a.m. and I think I can still do that. Guys, help me!"

"I think Naaz and Sameer will be there with you. And me, Mehul and Nayra will handle it from here," Aman said.

"Fine! I think we will go upstairs and you guys handle it downstairs." We all took our responsibilities. I went upstairs, Naaz and Sameer followed me. I tried to switch on the lights, but bad luck was following me. Lights were not working at all.

"Guys, I think we will have to work in the dark," I said. And before I could say anything else, Naaz switched on the torch light from her phone and said, "I think this should help."

"Yeah, great! I don't know when you'll grow up Naaz. We have to work on the entire terrace. And this light is not going to help us," I said.

"Guys, guys, guys! Please don't fight. I'll go downstairs and get the electrician. I'll just go and get him. Till then, Maan, please try to work in the light of the phone torch, please," Sameer said.

"Ya, thanks buddy." Sameer went downstairs and I turned back to Naaz. "Torch please," I asked her to switch on the torch in her phone.

"Please hold your phone properly so that I can get a good look. I can't even walk properly," I said.

"Can't you be quiet for some time? Look…" She offered me her phone and said, "Take this with you and I'll follow you."

I took the phone from her and told her, "Now see how we should hold the phone." Just then, I stumbled on something and I fell down on my back. Naaz tried to save me, but she didn't succeed, and fell over me. She started laughing after that. She was looking beautiful while laughing. Everything had stopped for me. I had a little smile pasted on my face while looking at her. But why the hell was she smiling in slow motion? I didn't want a slow motion, but a pause of a lifetime in that moment.

She continued laughing till she looked into my eyes. We were trying to understand the language of our eyes. We were just looking at each other. She closed her eyes and kept her lips on mine. Suddenly she jerked up and stood a few steps away, her back towards me. Then she went into some deep thoughts. I went near her and kept my hand on her shoulder. She removed my hand and walked a few more steps away from me.

"What the hell do you want, Naaz?" Every time, she did the same. And I was sure about it this time too. I didn't expect her to speak. She always ran away from situations. She walked towards the stairs.

"Wait, Naaz! Today you have to listen to me." She stopped there and I continued, "Why can't we talk about this, Naaz? This has become your habit, running away. You know how much I love you. I have spent so many sleepless nights thinking about you. But you don't care about my emotions at all. I want an answer, Naaz. You have to answer my all questions."

"What do you want, Maan? Wasn't a kiss enough for you?" Naaz turned to face me.

"What are you talking about Naaz? I love you and you know that. I have told you a thousand times."

"And what was my reply to you every single time?"

"You didn't say anything, but today I want the words out from you."

"I thought you are smart enough. I won't need to say anything and you'll understand everything by yourself." She was being straightforward. I could see that she was set out to spoil everything.

"What do you mean? Don't you have any feelings for me?"

She came near to me and held both my hands. Then she looked into my eyes and said, "Maan, I seriously don't have any feelings for you."

"Then what was all this? Let me remind you that we spent so many nights together and the matter did not end over there. You have just kissed me. I didn't force you. It was not one-sided, and you were equally involved. Please Naaz, I beg you, don't break my heart. I have loved you from the day that I met you. The thing is, I realized everything very late, Naaz."

"Late for what? Let's assume you were having feelings for me and you might have realized it late, but I never had those kind of feelings for you. Actually, I would say, I don't even understand what kind of feelings should be there?" She was trying to explain but I was unable to stop my tears.

"Don't do this to me, Naaz. I won't be able to live." I held her from the shoulders and said, "Look Naaz, just look into my eyes. I know you love me too; it's just that you don't realize that."

"Leave me, Maan, it's hurting."

"Just try to feel the love, Naaz." I tried to hug her.

Her anger burst out and she pushed me away and said, "Just stay in your limits, Maan. You just need sex and nothing else from me. Just come close and finish it."

I went near her and slapped her. "Mind your language. My love is pure, Naaz. And I think now you should leave. Now even I have understood that you don't have any feelings in your heart. Not just for me, but for anyone who cares about you."

"Thank god you understand that, Maan. Now I beg you to throw me out of your life. For me, it was just fun and nothing else, and maybe that's the reason why I was equally involved. I'm sorry

I made you feel like it was love. But let me tell you one thing – I think you should focus more on Kiara. She's pregnant, if you have forgotten. Please focus on her, she is a good woman. I'm leaving."

"I don't want your advice, Naaz. Please leave!" I sank to the floor saying that. Her fading steps confirmed that she was going away. Tears were flooding out of my eyes.

"Why did you do this to me?" I looked at the sky full of stars.

"Maan, please don't cry." Sameer was back to the terrace.

"Sameer, you don't know what happened just now."

"I know everything. I mean I heard everything standing behind the wall."

"Why did she do this to me?" I asked in a broken voice.

"Look at me, Maan. Just forget her and move on. There are many things to do in life. You have to accept the truth."

"Sometimes I think why the hell did god have to bring her in my life if he didn't want us to be together? Why I fell in love with only her, when it was sure that I was not going to get her? Why doesn't god want me to be happy? Was I born in this world just to be sad?"

"Look Maan, I know you are very hurt. And I know you won't be able to forget her. Even if you try, you won't be able to erase her completely from your life. I would say just think about Kiara, she is in the same situation where you were five minutes back. I mean, she doesn't know that you love her or not, and imagine, what if she comes to know that you don't love her at all? It's time to move on, Maan. And focus not only on Kiara, but on your child too." Sameer told me and calmed me down by wiping off my tears.

"Sameer, for some people, love comes twice or thrice or maybe more. Someone can realize the definition of true love in their life only when they find a particular person. For me, humans fall in love only once. You can say it is true love. You are right that I should take care of Kiara and my child. But the thing is, I won't be able to give them love at all. Naaz is set so well in my heart that nothing else will fit inside. And if you ask me, I still feel that Naaz loves me a lot. But something is stopping her. I don't know what it is, but something's there for sure. Earlier I was confused whether she loves me or not. But things are making it clear that she loves me." My voice became stable now.

"I don't know what I should do with you Maan. I was there, standing just behind the door. Accept that she doesn't love you at all. I can't see you like this. And I'm more worried about your married life. You are ruining your life," Sameer was very angry now.

"I'm ruining my life? Don't you think god is responsible for this all? And if you are asking about Kiara, let me make it clear that I do care for her and she is my responsibility, you need not be worried for her. There's only one way that all of us would be happy. Happiness would come only after my death. I'm not a coward that I'll kill myself or something like that. But I do pray for my death every day," I said.

"You know, god gives us everything we ask for, just the timing should be correct. And you know why you are still alive? It's not like god hasn't heard you, but he has heard me too. And I have always prayed for your long life, Maan," Kiara came from behind. She might have heard everything, or maybe not.

"We were just talking bullshit Kiara. When did you come here? And how did you know that we are here?" Sameer tried to cover up, assuming Kiara might not have heard everything.

"Sameer, I saw Naaz crying and running through the house. I thought something was wrong and saw you two here. I heard all your conversation." She came closer and Sameer made space in front of me. Kiara hugged me and said, "Your life might not be important for you or for someone else, but for me, you are more than my life." Her warm hug melted me and I wrapped my arms around her and hugged her back.

"But Kiara, I'm not good for you. I won't be able to love you. I love someone else. And it hasn't been only Naaz, there have been a few more," I said it without thinking of consequences. She was shocked but somehow made herself stable.

Wiping her tears, she said, "Don't you feel ashamed of yourself? You were not cheating only on me, but even Naaz. You don't deserve to be with anyone, not even Naaz. Maan, I trusted you. Those other girls include Jiah also, right?" I just nodded my head and she added, "That means I was right. I talked to my mother about it but she didn't believe me. She asked me to trust you. If you did not love me, then why did you give this child to me? Wasn't it enough to ruin only my life? You also involved our child in all this."

"Kiara please, don't take stress. Everything will be fine. Now onwards, he won't talk to Naaz. That's my guarantee. Can't you see he is all broken?" Sameer said.

"Guarantee? Even you didn't have faith on your friend. How you would give any guarantee," Kiara said.

"Sameer, she is absolutely right. I have cheated on her. I don't even deserve her in my life, or Naaz. I have cheated on them both."

"I'm sorry Maan, I don't think I would be able to live with you anymore. Till now, I lived with you with the hope that my love will change you. You'll forget Naaz and you'll choose me over her. But you proved me wrong. It's better to live alone than be humiliated in a relationship like this. I can take care of myself, Maan, I'm leaving. You should go back to Naaz."

"I'm sorry Kiara. I'm sorry. I won't stop you, because you are right. I know I won't be able to love you back. It would be good for both of you to stay away from a loser like me. But just allow me to see my child." Kiara didn't reply and went downstairs.

"I'm sorry Maan. But now, I don't think even I should stay here. I think you have to manage everything by yourself," Sameer said and went off.

Without raising her hand, Kiara had slapped me hard, and showed me the mirror of what I had done with her. I thought of ending my life there and then by jumping over the terrace. But I wanted to see god's worst plan for me. I spent a long time on the terrace. I saw everyone leaving one by one. Now it was only me and my parents when I went downstairs.

"What did you do?" Dad asked me.

"Dad, I didn't do it knowingly," I said.

"Don't you dare call me Dad. You have ruined my daughter Kiara's life. We won't forgive you for your sin. Even we are leaving this house." Dad looked at Mom and further told her, "Hand over the keys to him."

"Mom, I don't wants those keys. I want you guys. I can't live without you. Please, Mom. This empty house will kill me."

"Maan, I have to go with your Dad. I can't leave him alone. I can't leave my life partner alone, like you did. Sorry, but you have to live with your guilt because this time, you did mess up real bad." I tried to stop them. I begged them to stay. But they said they loved their daughter-in-law more than their son. They were all gone now, and it was just me staying at home. I kept crying all alone in my house. But I was not a coward. I decided to face every sin of mine. I would be cleaning the mess I had made of my life.

❖

"Don't you feel alone?" It had been close to one year, but Sameer was the only person who couldn't resist meeting me frequently.

"I have learned to live without everyone. Now I'm someone without a heart. Nothing can change me and nothing can make me cry. I'm waiting for Naaz. I haven't shared the news of my separation with her. I stopped talking to her, accepting that she doesn't love me," I said.

"That means you are over Naaz," Sameer said.

"No, I didn't say that. For me, Naaz is still everything. My love for her would never be less. It's just that I don't want to hurt her anymore. Every time I propose, she is hurt and I can't see that. And that's why I can only wait, nothing else. And now, all this doesn't affect me at all. I told you I have become stone-hearted now."

Sameer only nodded, what could he say! "Now I'm losing hope of even Naaz coming back to my life," I added.

"So, what now? Any plans?"

"I'm a successful businessman now. I don't think I need anything else in my life. I'm living my life, that's enough. You are with me. How can I be alone? Thank you Sameer, for being with me."

# 10

# Back Home

"You know Jigar, your story is confusing me. I mean, it doesn't feel real. Who can spend his or her life in the memory of a person who doesn't love them back?" Mona said after listening to Maan's story.

"Mona, I think it's easy to say that because we have not been in such a situation. Imagine me being in such a situation and put yourself in Kiara's shoes," I tried to explain her.

"If I find anything like that, you will find divorces papers instead of snacks on your dining table."

"Kiara did the same. She filed for divorce. And she got it within one year. I feel bad for Maan."

"Jigar, I think it's too late and I feel sleepy. We should sleep now," Mona said and stretched a blanket which was well-folded on the bed. She didn't look too keen on talking. Just after a few minutes, she suddenly woke up and said, "Hey Jigar! Please wake up, yaar."

"What's the matter Mona? Are you okay?"

"No, wake up! I need to talk to you. Now." She again pulled my blanket.

"What the hell Mona! Please yaar… Okay, tell me." I knew she won't allow me to sleep until she shared her so-called important thing.

"I think we should help Maan and Naaz to get together."

"Are you awake? I hope you are not talking in your sleep."

"God, no! I am fully awake and I was not sleeping at all," she threw a pillow at me and said.

"Okay okay. But I don't know them. How would I find the address and all? And don't you think even his friends would have tried to get them together?"

"First you finish the full story and then let me decide."

"I have told you the full story."

"Don't try to fool me. I know you are sleepy, but you have to tell me. If that was the end of the story, then Maan should have been happy when you met him at the airport. Instead of that, he was crying in the loo. He told you that he had become stone-hearted, then why was he crying. So definitely, there is something more."

"Yeah, you are right, there is something more. Even I asked the same question to him when he ended the story over there."

She had caught me. And I had to share the remaining story with her.

"Then why were you crying Maan? I mean your story seems to end over here," I asked Maan at the airport.

"My life hasn't been simple at all. Kiara really lived happily that whole year. We had a beautiful boy that year, the one you saw in the pictures. But my life was never going to be so easy and simple."

"What! You found another girl like Jiah or some colleague?" I asked him.

"No, no, no! After that incidence, I have never been in a relationship with anyone. I have been in control."

"Then what is the problem, Maan?" I was getting curious.

"If you won't ask more questions, I might speak."

"Okay, okay. Sorry, continue…"

"My fatherhood was not allowing me to stay away from my child. I used to go and see him every Saturday and Sunday at Kiara's place. Even my parents were living with her and they were happy that I still cared for them. Kiara had decided to live as a single parent for the rest of her life, and was managing it too. She was doing some job at an MNC with a good salary. Mom and Dad were helping her bring up my child. My dad was building hopes that we might get together. But I was sure I did not want to hurt Kiara again."

"That means you learned to deal with her?" I said.

"Yeah, kind of. But Kiara could not deal with that. My frequent visits were disturbing her. I had planned to visit my son today. She just called me and told me to stay away from her family. My loneliness was disturbing her a lot. According to her, our son was carrying wrong hopes of getting me in their life. I can handle any pain, but staying away from my child is not possible. But I have to do that. Now no more trouble for Kiara.

I have kept her in so much pain already. Now I want her to be in peace. And I have to pay my dues."

"Okay, now I get it," Mona said after listening to the remaining story.

"Okay, you got the point! So I think I should go to sleep now." I was really sleepy.

"I think we should help Maan. He is in trouble." She ignored my sentence completely.

"Again, the same thing? I told you I don't know them and you might have not listened… this is a one-sided love story. Naaz doesn't loves him at all."

"How can you be so sure?"

"Arey, Maan told me. That he has proposed to her many times but she always refused to answer."

"Refusing to answer doesn't mean she did not love him."

"But once she answered in a no, when they met on the terrace, remember?" I argued with her.

"I do not count that as an answer," she said.

"Okay, let's assume that you are right, but don't you think that his best friends might have tried to help him? I think they did not succeed in getting them together."

"Yeah, but listening to your story and being a woman, I can say that his friends only made one-sided efforts. I don't think any of them went to Naaz. I think we should approach her. And specifically, when Naaz refused his proposal, he was married. Now he is not. I don't think Naaz knows anything about it." Actually she was making sense, even past midnight.

"But the question is, I don't know them, especially Naaz. I have seen Maan and heard him, nothing else. But I have his contact number. I don't think he will give me Naaz's contact."

"You will always be confused. I didn't ask you to call Maan."

"Then what should I do? I think right now I should sleep."

"Grow up man! I am talking about social media. You are really a person with old thoughts. Just stand up and give me your laptop," she again ignored my last sentence. I got up and gave her my laptop.

"Listen, have you seen Maan or Naaz? Or any of their family members?"

"No, I don't think so. But I have seen Maan."

"Oh, thank you, you at least know that." Then she turned the laptop to me and showed me the suggestions provided by Facebook on searching his name. There were plenty of options and I was getting confused.

"Can you open this profile?" I told her and immediately added, "No, no, no. This is not him."

This happened a good three or four times.

"Have you seen him or not?" She was getting angry now.

"I have, but it has been long and we only met once. You just scroll down, let me see some more." She started scrolling down but I was unable to recognise.

"I think we should sleep now. And I'll try it in morning. I can't do this anymore."

"Go to hell, you useless fellow." Finally she approved and let me sleep. She shut down the laptop and took her place beside me.

"Your tea is ready Jigar. Wake up!" she called out to me and I sleepily walked to the dining room. A laptop was kept on the table, waiting for my hands to work on it.

"I think you haven't come out of Maan yet," I said rubbing my eyes.

"Just go and check the laptop first. I think I found him," she said with a smile and I hurried to look.

"Yes, this is Maan! But you haven't even seen him; how did you find him?"

"You told me that you have his contact number. I just searched him on WhatsApp and found his picture. Then I woke up early and found this profile."

"You are great. But now what?"

"Just send him a friend request."

"Is he going to accept your friend request?"

"That's your Facebook account, hubby," she said

"How do you know my login ID and password?"

"I know everything about you, like Kiara knows everything about Maan."

"You women are really impossible!"

"Can you please send a friend request, so that we can find Naaz from his profile?"

"What if he doesn't accept?"

"Why you are always so negative?"

"Okay, okay I'm sending." Seriously, it's hard to fight with women. I sent a request and went to work. It was a hard day for me, having joined after a vacation. I came back home after completing a lot of pending work and guess what I found on the dining table!

"A laptop! Mona, I'm not in mood to find Naaz or anyone else. Please… I'm tired."

"You don't have to find anyone, I already found Naaz. You just get ready for next week and inform your staff to take care of the office for a few days."

"For what?"

"I have booked our tickets for Indore and then from there to Kerala."

"Cancel the tickets right now. I have some very important meetings."

"I'm not asking you. Just go and pack your bags! This Saturday, we are leaving for Indore. Naaz is still in Indore."

"Indore is not a small city, how will we find her?"

"She has written where she works. So I think it would be easy for us to find her workplace."

She had thought this through. I realised I had no option but to go with her. And Mona had booked the train tickets already.

❖

"Seriously? I don't believe we are doing this." I was frustrated with the long journey.

We were having this argument again in the train.

"You are making new friends, then you come to me and share their story with me, and you know me well. I do my best to help people."

"This is not called helping people; this is called madness. You can also call this interfering in someone's life. I don't know what I'm doing here with you," I said. I don't know why but people around us were taking too much interest in our conversation.

"What's wrong? Don't you guys have any other work to do?" My wife shouted at them and came to me. "Look, Jigar! Stop making anonymous friends and if you want to do that, just make sure you don't share their story with me."

"I just don't understand your theory at all. When I wasn't sharing anything with you, you had a problem. And now when I'm sharing something with you, you still have a problem. I don't know what to do!" Thank god I was not at home and I knew she would not shout or act up in front of so many people.

"Look Jigar, I don't want to argue with you. I just know you don't have it in you to help anybody, so I took the first step." Our fight was not stopping at all. And the people around us were enjoying it.

In a few hours, we reached Indore. Mona took her phone out and gave me the address to find on Google map. I found the location and we took a cab.

"I don't understand why you take so much luggage with you all the time," I said stuffing the big bags into the cab.

"Now you have problem with my luggage too? Seriously, I don't understand where you find all these topics to argue over."

"Topics? How can you say that? I mean look at you, you are sitting in the cab and I'm handling the bags. And your bag is the heaviest one."

"If you are finished, just get into the car. I have explained the address to the driver." This was Mona's forte, she never finished her arguments.

When we reached, I paid the cabbie for the trip and we entered the building. It was a commercial building, fully covered with reflecting glass. If you see it from the top, it will look oval. It also contained a small fountain in the foyer. We saw the name plates on one of the walls, and Mona found her company. We took the lift for the seventh floor. We entered her office and saw a beautiful receptionist.

"Hello ma'am, how can I help you?" she asked my wife.

"Hi! Actually we want to meet Naaz. She works here," I said before Mona could start talking. Mona gave me a weird look, like I had done something wrong.

"What? Stop giving me that look!" I said.

"Please don't mind him. Can you please tell me where we can find her?" my wife said.

"Ma'am, there are two Naazs here. Can you give me her full name?"

"I think it's Naaz Siddiquie," Mona said.

"Have you taken an appointment?" We shook our head and she added "Just give me your name I will ask her."

She dialled a number and turned her face to one of the cabins. Maybe Naaz occupied that cabin. There were small horizontal lines on the frosted glass, through which we could see small bits. And since it was too quiet, I could hear Naaz's voice too.

"Ma'am, two people are here to meet you, Mrs and Mr Prajapati," the receptionist said.

"Is there an appointment marked for them?"

"No, ma'am."

"Okay, tell them to come tomorrow. I'm a bit busy today."

The moment we heard this, Mona started trying to convince her that we had come from far off to meet her and all. But she was not convinced. I don't know what happened to me but I ran towards Naaz's cabin. And when my wife saw me, even she ran behind me.

"Sir, ma'am, please stop!" The receptionist shouted. We both entered her cabin and locked the glass door from inside.

Naaz started shouting heavily.

"Ma'am please don't shout, we won't harm you. We just want to talk." We tried to go near her and calm her down.

"Don't you dare come near me." She looked really scared. I never knew we looked that dangerous.

"Okay, okay! We won't. Just calm down!" I said.

"You open the door first."

"We will open the door, but please just listen to us."

"I won't listen to you unless you open the door." Not seeing any other way out, I went and unlocked the door.

Naaz observed that and said, "Now stand away from the door."

We both did that but Naaz started shouting again.

"Security, security…"

"Please listen to us. We won't harm you. We just want to talk about something," I tried to explain, but she was not in mood to listen.

She continued shouting. A few guards entered her cabin and they held us from behind.

"Ma'am, we want to talk about Maan," Mona said.

As soon as Naaz heard Maan's name, she asked her guards to wait.

"What did you just say?"

"Actually we have come here to talk about Maan," I said trying to maintain some calm.

"You can leave them," she directed the guards, but quickly added, "Stay outside and wait for my sign."

"Thank you, Naaz." My wife said and Naaz offered us to have our seats opposite her.

"So, what do you guys want to talk about? Is there any message from Maan? Is he alright?" Naaz said.

"Yes, I love you," I said in a hurry.

"You guys are impossible! I think she is your wife and you are using those words in front of her. I think both of you should leave now. Just get out!"

She was just about to throw us out when my wife interrupted her and said, "I apologize on his behalf."

Then she turned at me and said, "Will you just keep your mouth shut for a while? You will get us thrown out, silly."

"You are right," Naaz told Mona. "Why don't you sit on the sofa?" Naaz got comfortable with Mona and offered me a seat a few steps away from the table.

"Now just make sure you don't speak a word," my wife said.

I stood up from the chair and went straight to the sofa. Both of them were observing me. I took my place and was waiting for them to talk. But they were still staring at me.

"What? Are you waiting for me to speak? I thought you were supposed to talk," I shouted. Both of them ignored my last sentence and they started their conversation.

"Naaz, my husband met Maan at the airport. He shared his story with Jigar," Mona said.

"I don't know any Jigar. I mean, I know every friend of Maan. He shared everything with me," Naaz said.

"My husband's name is Jigar. And Maan and Jigar are not friends. It's just that they met at the airport and Maan shared his story with him."

"I have a hunch that you guys are fooling me," Naaz said.

"Naaz, leave all this. Let's just get to the point. You have to believe us Naaz, and if you can't do that, we do have our train for return," Mona said.

"Okay, go ahead!"

"Naaz, Maan loves you a lot. He is not able to forget you," Mona said and I was just staring at their faces and observing their reactions.

"Okay, I got your message. You guys can leave now," Naaz said.

"You really can't face the truth, right?"

"Truth? What do you know about me and Maan?"

"I don't know much about you, but I'm sure that even you love Maan. I am a woman too. I do know how we express our feelings. Maan has told you thousands of times that he loves you, but you didn't even respond. How can you be so heartless, Naaz?"

"I had already rejected his proposal. People like you have filled his mind with love, which is ruining our friendship too."

"People like us? What do you know about us? I mean, have you even asked our names?"

"I don't know and I don't even want to know. I have got your message and tell Maan that I don't love him at all. And tell him to stop sending stupid messengers like you, who do not even have the sense to talk."

"Done, Mona? Now I can't listen to anything worse than this." I turned to Naaz. "You know, I told her this is a one-sided love story and nothing else. But no! She wanted to do some social work. Let's make some good work and get Maan and Naaz together. Their short form would also look good 'Maanaaz'. My foot! Mona she does not have feelings at all. You know what, let Maan die. I think his last wish to meet Naaz won't be possible. Let's just move from here." Mona was not ready to go out but I held her hand and took her towards the door.

"Wait a minute! Is there any problem? Is Maan in danger? What happened to him?" Naaz stood up from her place and asked us many questions in one line.

"Why should we tell you anything? Who are you? Do you even care about him? And we are nonsense, foolish people. Why should you even listen to us?"

"Fine! Just go! I'll ask Maan," she said.

"Fine, just call. No one is going to answer. I don't think people in ICU are allowed to take calls," Mona said. She had understood my trick and was on the right track.

"ICU?" She kept her hand on her face and ran towards us. "Please tell me what happened?"

"Again I have the same question – why should we share anything with you? You don't even love him," I said.

"I don't love him? There's no one in this world who loves him more than I do." She burst out and added, "I have been dying for him."

She started walking back to her chair and continued talking, "When he proposed for the first time, I was not sure about love and all that. But I was more scared about what would happen if my parents found out about my love for Maan. I mean, I am a Muslim girl and my father would have never accepted us. I thought it was just attraction, and nothing else. I did not believe anything like love exists.

"Just a few days later, I came to know that he was getting married to a girl named Kiara. She was very beautiful and charming. He again dared to confess his love to me before he was getting married to Kiara. But I thought he would forget me after he got married. But no, he didn't forget me. Instead of that, he started loving me more. Every time he proposed, I tried not to answer him, but he didn't stop. He kept on doing that. Even at his wife's baby shower, I tried to stay away from him. But he came to me and again professed his love. And at that time, he forced me to speak. And I rejected his proposal. How could I accept his proposal Mona? He was going to be a father. What was Kiara's fault in all this? Why should she suffer?" She started crying after saying all that.

"Naaz, please stop crying." Mona went to her and hugged her to calm her down a bit.

"Please tell me what's wrong with Maan?" She joined her hands and requested us to say something.

I went close to her and said, "Nothing has happened to him. He is well. We just wanted to know whether you love him or not."

She cried for a few more minutes after knowing Maan was okay. She took back her chair some minutes later and said, "Okay guys, you have succeeded. Now you guys can go home. Thank you very much."

"You think we were here just to know your feelings? We already knew that you love him. We just wanted to hear it from you, Naaz. Don't take us wrong, but we want you two to be together. We want you to come with us to Kerala and tell Maan that you love him." Mona took the lead.

"Thank you guys, you at least thought for us. But I don't think I should do that. I can't ruin Kiara's life."

"You have already done that, Naaz." Mona's words shocked Naaz. "Kiara knows everything about you and Maan. She has been wishing that you get back into Maan's life. She can't see Maan crying and praying for death. They are not together now, they got divorced about a year back. And now, Maan is all alone. He is just praying for just one thing – his death."

"Praying for what?"

"Yes Naaz, he thinks after his death, everything will be okay. Everyone's life will be happy after a few days of sadness. These are his thoughts, and generally, elders say that whatever you ask from god, he gives it to you – sooner or later. I think Maan is a good person and he does not deserve to be in this condition. He deserves something beautiful… something like you Naaz," I said.

"He's right. Just give yourself a chance in love. If you are worrying about Kiara, then let me tell you that she would be happy in Maan's happiness. She won't have any problem. Maan is not able to meet his child nowadays, because Kiara doesn't want their child to see such a melancholy version of his father," Mona said.

"Why didn't he share anything with me?" Naaz said.

"He was afraid he would hurt you. Every time he proposed, you got hurt. And now he did not want that. Hurting you was hurting him too," I said.

Naaz did not say anything. She stared at a wall for a few seconds and was not even wiping off her tears. She just turned to her landline and called the receptionist.

"Do one thing for me. Just book three flight tickets to Kerala. The other two names are Jigar and Mona Prajapati."

"We already have our train tickets booked for Kerala. Please tell her to book only your ticket," Mona said.

"Actually she is scared of planes. So, we hardly travel by air," I said.

"You have come so far ahead, and I can't let you back off now guys. You can take that much risk for us, Mona? Please," Naaz said.

"Of course, why not!" she said but I knew she wanted to refuse. And now I was going to suffer a lot. I was going to have scars on my hands. But I was happy that Naaz and Maan were going to be together and all credit goes to my wife, Mona. So, I was okay to bear those scars for a few hours.

We landed in Kerala the next day. Naaz was carrying a bigger bag than Mona.

"Please Naaz, my husband is here. He'll take the entire luggage. I think we should go out and book a taxi," Mona said. Was she out of her mind? I just wanted to kill this woman.

"Are you sure, Jigar? You don't need any help, right? And what's wrong with your hands?"

"You are talking about these scars? They are Mona's passionate love for me." She laughed and went outside the airport with Mona. I looked at the luggage. I brought a trolley and one by one, loaded the luggage on it. My luck is always opposing me. The trolley was too hard to move forward, but I slowly took it out and kept the luggage in a cab.

"Why are you sweating so much?" Mona asked.

"Nothing I just took a round of the airport. You told me that I should go for exercise and I just started that."

She ignored me completely and instead, started talking to Naaz. Naaz knew where Maan was working and she gave the address of his workplace to the cabbie. It was 9.30 a.m. and Google showed that we would reach our destination by 10 a.m.

"What if Maan is on leave today?" I said.

"Just shut up! You are always negative," Mona said. I realised it was better to stay silent.

"No, but I think we can get his address from his office," Naaz said.

We were lost in the beauty around us. The driver was driving a bit too fast for my comfort but since the women didn't point it out, I stayed quiet too. Then, the driver suddenly lost control and had to steer the car into a small lane to save us from bumping into another vehicle. Sadly, the cab hit a biker coming from the other side of the lane. He and his bike had slipped a few metres away from us. The driver got scared and tried to drive off.

"Driver, stop the car! We need not to run. It was not our fault at all. That person needs our help," Naaz said.

All three of us went out and saw that he was bleeding a lot.

"Guys, we need to take him to the hospital," Mona said.

"Is there any hospital nearby?" Naaz asked the taxi driver.

"Yes, there is, but I won't take him in my taxi."

"I'll pay you double. You have to help us," Naaz said and the driver agreed.

"We have to remove his helmet. Naaz, you help me ," I said. Both of us removed his helmet.

"Oh my god, Maan! Wake up! He is not responding." Naaz started crying.

"Naaz, this is not the time to cry. Let's get him to the hospital. His breathing is slow, but steady. You have to be strong," I said trying to rush things.

"Maan, you can't leave me now," Naaz said.

Listening to her voice, Maan opened his eye and looked at Naaz. He was unable to say anything but he smiled at Naaz and went unconscious. We took him to a nearby hospital. We reached the emergency ward and Maan was handed over to the doctors. I finished all the formalities while Mona stayed with Naaz.

"Naaz, you have to call Kiara," I said.

"No, I can't tell her," she said.

"Look Naaz, you have to call her. We don't know Kiara. So, it would be better if you make a call." Things were complicated here. Naaz gathered courage and called up Kiara. She gave the news in her broken voice and also shared the hospital details. Kiara reached the hospital in just ten minutes. She came to us and took all the detail. We all were waiting. After half an hour, the inner door opened and a doctor stepped out. All four of us ran to him to know what was happening.

"Sorry, we couldn't save him," was all he said. Listening to these words, Kiara sat down on the floor and started screaming. All three of us took Kiara to the seating area and gave her some water. We let her cry, what else could we do?

I went and completed the formalities to take the body. In a few minutes, some police officers entered the hospital. They asked me everything about the accident. They even asked Kiara whether she wanted to file an FIR against the driver. She refused, saying it was an accident, and she did not want to press charges. The hospital van was ready to take Maan's body home.

Mona climbed into the van with Kiara. Naaz was about to climb in, but Kiara stopped her.

"Please Naaz, I respect you, but I don't want you to enter the van. You weren't with him when he was alive, so you don't have the right to be with him when he is no more." Naaz was already so broken that I did not know how she would take this news.

"You come with me in that taxi. We will just follow them," I said. She followed me without a word. This was life's most difficult situation, at least for me. I always run out of words when someone is so broken. I decided to keep quiet. We followed the van and reached the house. People were already waiting, some old and some young. I presumed his parents were also there.

"Jigar, could you please help me in putting some stuff in that car?" Kiara showed me a car which was parked in one corner of the house. I just nodded my head and followed her. She didn't meet anyone and directly went inside the house. It looked like she was collecting some things – clothes, some awards and some accessories.

"Whose bag are you packing?" I asked to put an end to the suspense.

"Maan's. His parents have decided to stay in their own house. They want to donate Maan's things."

I took all the boxes with me and kept them in the car. An envelope fell out from one of the boxes. I picked it up and opened it. It was a letter.

*It feels like I wasted my life's precious time to hear a yes from you,*

*You always rejected my proposal, but I did not lose hope,*
*The air between us was saying that you love me,*
*Your shining eyes were saying that you love me,*
*I'm waiting for your lips to say something,*
*I'm waiting for your hands to hold my hands,*
*Something is stopping you for sure,*
*Maybe society, maybe your parents,*
*Maybe your ego, maybe your religion,*
*Maybe god stopped you…*
*I'm clear from my side that I have always loved you,*
*I still love you, and I always will.*
*Nobody on earth can stop me from loving you,*
*Hope is never going to end,*
*It's just that I'm waiting for one word – Yes.*

"Maan wrote this letter for Naaz. He just couldn't post it. He told me that one day he'll give it to her." Kiara came from behind and told me.

"Then why not now?"

"Naaz does not have feelings for Maan at all. Even this letter won't bring any change to her. I don't think we should give it to her."

"That's not the truth, Kiara. May be you don't know, but I met Maan at the airport a couple of days back. He told me his whole story and my wife forced me to meet Naaz. There she admitted that even she loved Maan. Just because he was married, she stayed away, so that you guys can be happy. We told her that your happiness is in Maan's happiness. And you both are separated now. We brought her to Kerala so that she could share her feelings with Maan. But god had decided something else."

Kiara took that letter from my hand and went to Naaz. Kiara slapped Naaz so hard that I went numb for a minute.

"How could you, Naaz? How could you? All your life you thought about me? I was no one, Naaz. He always loved you. He was dying to hear your voice. I know what he has gone through in his life. You are too late, Naaz. Just take this letter Maan had written for you. I want you to regret what you did for the rest of your life." She threw the letter on her face and went back to his family.

Mona and I looked at each other. We were not able to do anything now. God has decided their destiny.

"Naaz, we are really sorry for your loss. Hope you'll spend life in peace. Also, I pray to god that his soul rests in peace. Just take care of yourself Naaz. We are leaving; we have our train for tomorrow." Mona consoled Naaz. She did the same with Kiara too.

❖

We caught our train the next day. We usually fight at each and every moment, but yesterday's incident brought silence upon us. We both were in deep thoughts.

"I love you, Mona," I said.

"What happened to you?"

"I didn't expect this reply. But you would be thinking why I'm saying this, right? Just because I don't want to be late like Naaz. Mona, I think we should share our thoughts without wasting time, without being worried about the result."

"You are right. You know what, after a long time, we are having a sensible conversation. By the way, I love you too. And I think we should not fight anymore. I just didn't like the scenario and that's killing me. We don't know them. We just met them only once. I should not get such sad feelings, right? But I feel like I'm attached to them."

"Even I'm going through the same feelings. I know why we feel like that… maybe because Maan could not come to know that Naaz really loved him. Maybe more than he loved Naaz," I said.

"Perhaps you are right, but I think we did our best to help them. And we even learned something from them. The rest was just destiny."

"Yeah, they made me say the things I have never said to you,"I said.

"Not only you, they made me do that too." We hugged each other and felt bad for Naaz and Maan.

"You have gained some weight," I said.

"Have you seen your tummy?"

"That's because I have to eat outside food."

"Who has stopped you from eating homemade food?"

"I'll eat after you learn to cook."

"I'm not going to talk to you."

Our fights were never going to end. Just like our story.

●●●